I0757545

PAN AFRICAN
LIFESTYLE

AKEEM MALEEK

AND THE

CROWN OF ALKEBULAM

A FANTASY NOVEL

BY

EMMANUEL BOPE and SOLANGE BOPE

Canada

Pan African Lifestyle Inc.

Copyright © 2021

PAN AFRICAN LIFESTYLE INC.

All rights reserved. No part of this book may be reproduced in any form without written permission from Pan African Lifestyle Inc. Quotes of brief texts are permitted for educational and media-related dialogue and reviews.

Authors: Emmanuel Bope and Solange Bope

Editors: John D. Beloved & Cassandra Tyrone

Contributing Author: Cassandra Tyrone

Printed and bound in Calgary, AB, CANADA

First printing July 2024

Published by Pan African Lifestyle Inc.

ISBN 978-1-998780-15-0   Paperback

panafricanlifestyle.com

DEDICATION

With deepest gratitude, we thank God Almighty,
whose boundless mercy and divine wisdom lit the
path before us and sustained our hearts, minds, and
hands through every chapter of this journey.
To love.
To friendship that stands the test of time,
and to partners in both life and purpose,
whose patience, grace, and steadfast companionship
were the quiet force behind every page.
But above all, this book is for you; our beloved Pan-
African readers across the globe, from the vibrant
corners of the diaspora to the sacred soil of the conti-
nent. You who have yearned for a tale that reflects
our spirit, our roots, and The African Dream.
May the journey of Akeem Maleek awaken
something ancient and noble within you.
May it remind you of who you are
and what you come from.
For you are the story.
And we are because you are.
Ubuntu.

EPIGRAPH

In Memoriam

Lest we forget the millions of lives lost in the Democratic Republic of Congo, and the silent genocide that continues to unfold against the Congolese people—a tragedy too often ignored, too seldom named.
In the words of the martyred hero, **Patrice Lumumba***:*
"History will have its say one day. Not the history they teach in Brussels, Paris, Washington or the United Nations, but the history taught in the country set free from colonialism and its puppet rulers. Africa will write her own history, and it will be a history of glory and dignity."
We echo that promise.
With unflinching resolve, we stand with the people of the Congo, Sudan, Haiti, and all African and diasporic nations confronting injustice. We stand against the unchecked greed of Big Tech, the exploitation of multinationals, the violence of capitalism, and the enduring grip of neocolonialism and imperialism.
We bear witness to the pillaging of sacred lands, and to the betrayal of our people by those who serve foreign interests at the cost of African lives and liberation.
But the tides are shifting.
The world will soon reckon with the awakening of Africa, and the renaissance of the diaspora and the continent; in dignity, in sovereignty, and in power.

CONTENTS

NOTE

In today's hyperconnected world, technology, particularly the rise of social media, has brought us closer together, allowing us to witness, share, and celebrate the uniqueness of our cultures while recognizing the deep threads that connect our collective heritage and experience. Social media has also exposed long-buried truths. Chief among them is the glaring absence of authentic Black narratives within mainstream media. Though people of African descent have shaped every corner of global culture, our stories are too often erased, appropriated, or flattened into harmful stereotypes.

Now more than ever, it is clear that we, the global Black community, must reclaim the narrative. Our stories must be written by us and for us, not merely to meet a quota for diversity, but to honor the full spectrum of our history, creativity, and lived experience. Through storytelling, our oldest and most powerful art form, we preserve our truths, inspire future generations, and shape a world that sees and celebrates us.

This realization set us on a journey, an imaginative, daring, and deeply personal one, to write a fantasy novel that not only entertains, but also educates, heals, and empowers. *Akeem Maleek and The Crown of Alkebulan* was born from that longing, for a story that truly sees us, that loves us, and that reflects the boundless excellence we are destined to manifest. A story that speaks with the voice of our ancestors and dreams with the language of our children. This is not just a fantasy novel, it is a Pan-African offering.

We follow Akeem Maleek, a brilliant young man from Atlanta, on the cusp of adulthood as he prepares for his graduation from an HBCU. But everything changes when three mysterious Magi arrive bearing a golden necklace, and a truth that alters the course of his life. Thrust into the hidden kingdom of Alkebulan, a breathtaking African superpower rich in history, technology, and spiritual force, Akeem finds himself at the crossroads of destiny.

What begins as a disruption becomes a sacred calling. As he uncovers his royal lineage, navigates betrayal, and confronts a legacy far greater than he imagined, Akeem must rise, not just as a leader, but as a symbol of unity, hope, and restoration. Along the way, love blooms, courage is tested, and purpose takes root.

We acknowledge the ongoing debate among scholars regarding the etymology of "Alkebulan," often cited as one of the oldest known names for Africa. For the purposes of this story, Alkebulan represents a fictional Central African superpower, a spiritual and political metaphor for a united, self-determined Africa.

In honor of Kwame Nkrumah and Ghana's "Year of Return," we have incorporated the rich symbolism of the Adinkra system to guide this narrative. Each chapter begins with an Adinkra symbol that anchors its central theme. Swahili, the most widely spoken language across Africa, serves as the national language of Alkebulan. These were deliberate choices, to honor, to unify, and to reimagine the continent through a Pan-African lens that embraces North, South, East, West, and Central Africa as one.

This story is ours. Every page, every sentence, is a reclamation. By weaving together elements of pop culture, ancestral memory, and futuristic fantasy, we hope to awaken the storyteller within each reader, across the diaspora and on the continent. Akeem Maleek's journey is a reminder that you, too, carry a royal legacy, one they never wanted you to discover.

This book is more than a novel. It is a bridge. It is a map. It is a crown. May you wear it well. For those who have long waited to see themselves in the pages of majesty and mythology, your time has come.

Welcome to Alkebulan.

PROLOGUE

The story of Akeem Maleek begins about twenty-five years before his birth.

The scent of ash clung to the air like a curse. The night was thick with screams, and the palace of Alkebulan, once a place of music and peace, was now reduced to smoke and chaos.

Queen Malaika awoke to rough hands shaking her from sleep. Her eyes fluttered open to the firelight flickering across the tense face of her husband, King Jabari. He wore no crown, and that absence made the moment feel all the more fragile.

"What's happening?" She breathed out.

A scream tore through the halls, closer this time.

"Muovu is here," Jabari said, voice tight. "Someone betrayed us. We must leave."

Even as he spoke, he was already lifting her from their acacia wooden four-poster bed, his gaze falling to her swollen belly.

She understood immediately. "Those traitors will pay for their insolence."

He paused, cupping her face, resting his forehead gently against hers. Her husband—the man whose strength had always calmed her storms—was trembling.

"Ndio, their time is coming," he murmured. "But not tonight. Tonight, we survive."

They needed no more words. They moved like seasoned warriors, with Jabari pulling a deep purple robe from the rack and wrapping it around her shoulders. It did little against the smoke, but it carried her mother's scent, giving her something to hold onto.

In the room stood nine guards—three by the chamber door, six more standing by a veiled panel behind a curtain. The royal chamber held secrets known only to the bloodline and its loyal defenders. Tonight, those secrets would become salvation. One pressed a hand to a hidden seal, and a section of the stone wall slid open, revealing a narrow passage lit by torchlight that spread along the walls.

Jabari gripped her hand as they moved forward. Each step pressed the weight of her unborn child deeper into her spine. Still, she walked.

Their descent was silent, save for the crackling flames above and the small, sharp gasps Malaika tried not to let become sobs.

Above them, the palace burned. General Muovu, once a brother-in-arms to Jabari, had turned traitor. His forces had breached the gates, and the last loyal warriors fought valiantly, but Muovu had an army. And soon, the fire would consume everything.

It was the reason why Jabari only took nine men he trusted. Of them, only two he believed would die for the crown without hesitation: his and Malaika's personal guards, who had been with them since the coronation.

A soft whimper escaped Malaika's lips.

"We're almost there," Jabari whispered, though the strain in his voice betrayed him.

They moved through the narrow passage until one of the guards ahead pressed open a hidden door and checked the path beyond. A quick nod signaled that it was clear.

Jabari tightened his grip on Malaika's hand and led her forward. Sweat traced her brow. She was close — perhaps too close — to giving birth.

The door opened into a secluded section of the royal garden, a place where only the royal bloodline walked. Tall trees arched above them, their canopies trembling in the wind, and waiting beneath them were three figures. The Magi, older than time itself, though they seemed not a day over 200.

At the center stood a tall man — called the Wise One — with skin as dark as the midnight sky, cloaked in indigo robes, a staff in hand, its crystal orb pulsing with golden light. The only color that marked him was his beard, strikingly white, cascading down like a waterfall of snow. At his sides were two others, standing still.

"It is time, your majesties," said the man called Shabazz. "We have been expecting you."

Jabari stepped in front of Malaika, hand resting protectively on her shoulder, his jaw tight.

"You told us we would defeat Muovu," he murmured, "but why are we fleeing in the dark like cowards?"

He remembered the prophecy well: "A traitor shall rise from within, casting down the throne and inviting chaos. Yet from the ashes, the royal line shall rise above all."

He had believed those words—had built his defenses around them and ignored the cracks splitting his kingdom. But Muovu had been smarter, spreading poison, and many had listened. And now, they were running.

Shabazz spoke again. "The prophecy gives what it can, and we interpret as best we know how —"

"You said we would take the kingdom back from him," Jabari snapped. "That was the point."

From the Magi's left, the smallest of the three, Amani, stepped forward. Though diminutive, he exuded confidence, and his wit had long endeared him to Malaika. He was the only one Jabari had come close to trusting.

"What the Wise One means," Amani said gently, "is that we saw the royal family reclaiming the palace. But the vision never said when."

Before Jabari could reply, the third Magi, Kwame, stepped forward. His face was grim.

"And there's more," he murmured. "We received another vision today."

Jabari's stomach turned. But it was Malaika who spoke first.

"Will my baby be safe?" She cradled her belly as if she could shield the unborn child from fate itself.

Shabazz held her gaze for a long moment. Then he nodded. "Everyone will be fine."

It wasn't the answer Malaika wanted, but there was no time to press further. A low rumble rolled beneath their feet, and then came the crash of stone collapsing.

"We need to leave now!" Shabazz commanded, lifting his staff as the orb blazed green.

The Magi moved quickly, surrounding the royal couple. "Form the circle!" Amani called.

Jabari wrapped his arms around Malaika, shielding her as she clutched her belly. The air swirled, and leaves lifted and spun around them. And then, silence.

They opened their eyes. They were no longer in the garden.

Sand stretched in all directions. The sky was grey, the landscape of sand a burnt orange, and the sunlight almost rosy despite the stone-grey clouds. The wind here was calmer, but the danger had only shifted, not vanished. Muovu would follow. He was cunning and knew the palace better than anyone, and worse, he knew the Magi's ways.

"The ship will be here soon," said Shabazz.

Before the royal couple could respond, rumblings from the ground seemed to shake heavier than an earthquake. From the earth emerged a dark silver ship with a glowing purple underglow. Then, the doors opened. They made their way toward it quickly, their footsteps muffled by the sand.

Jabari didn't wait. "You said there was another prophecy. What was it?"

Shabazz didn't flinch. "Not another. An extension of the first."

"Then speak it."

The Wise One looked ahead, as if reading the words from the sky. "The fruit of the royal family shall disrupt the enabler of chaos and bear the burden that is to come, if he allows it."

Malaika stopped, and so did they.

"My child will face Muovu? She gripped her belly, breathing hard. "What else? Tell me the rest."

But there was no rest. The prophecy had ended there. It had spoken of no victory or no defeat. Only the warning.

A tear slid down Malaika's cheek. Jabari wiped it gently, though his own hands were shaking. There were no words that could soften what had just been said. Only the knowledge that they stood at the edge of something terrible and that he had to carry her away from it.

"Don't worry, Laika," he whispered. "I'll protect you. I swear it. Nothing's going to happen to you. Not while I'm breathing. Let's go."

They turned toward the vessel. Took one step and froze as sounds split the night, like cracks in the air. They all turned around.

Three portals tore open behind them, spinning white rings. And from inside, long lines of light—lasers—shot out, slicing through the sand.

"They found us!" Jabari yelled.

The royal guards ran forward, dodging the beams. The first guard leapt across the sand and swung his spear, slicing the leg of one soldier emerging from a portal. Another guard tackled a second soldier, driving a blade into his side. But more were coming.

Jabari turned to Malaika. Her hand gripped his like it was the only solid thing left in the world.

"We need to move!" Shabazz shouted.

But Jabari didn't follow. Instead, he pressed a kiss to Malaika's forehead.

"Go with them! I'll be right behind you!"

Her eyes widened in horror. "No. We're not leaving you!"

Behind them, the guards were being pushed back. The enemy dressed in black armor advanced quickly. One lifted a weapon and fired, sending a guard flying.

"Do something!" Malaika screamed at the Magi. "Aren't you supposed to have powers?"

Shabazz fervently shook his head. "Our energy is holding the gate! If we fight, it collapses and we all die!"

"No, please!" She cried.

Jabari took her hands again, firmer this time.

"If I don't stay, none of you will get out. I need you to live for our son."

Tears streamed down her cheeks, like the falls of Mosi-oa-Tunya. "But when will you come back?"

He didn't respond to that. "Name him Akeem. Make him strong. You know how."

He kissed her one last time, as if trying to brand the memory into his soul. Then he turned without another word and ran into the fight.

Malaika screamed, her legs nearly giving way.

Amani caught her, pulling her toward the vessel. "We must go. Now!"

As the door sealed shut, she caught one last glimpse through the narrow slit.

Jabari was now standing before Muovu.

He struck the bigger man across the jaw, but he countered fast, kicking Jabari's legs. Jabari fell but quickly rose, jabbing forward, but Muovu blocked it with his forearm and kicked him hard in the chest. Jabari stumbled, sand flying behind him.

Still, he didn't stop.

He ran again and tackled Muovu to the ground. But it was no use. Muovu broke free. He raised his elbow and drove it down.

Jabari barely rolled aside. Blood and sweat blurred his vision. Around him, the last of his guards fell. There was no doubt now. He wouldn't survive.

From above, the scene shrank as the vessel lifted. Inside, Malaika collapsed, but the worst wasn't over. Her water broke.

Screams filled the chamber as pain seized her. The Magi rushed to her, their hands glowing as they tried to ease the agony, but it was more than pain. She cried out again, pushing through grief, fury, and sorrow until a cry rose that wasn't hers.

A boy.

The Magi placed the tiny bundle in her arms.

His skin was like hers—rich, deep brown. His eyes, wide and dark, blinked up at her. And though her body was breaking, his tiny smile reached the deepest part of her. She kissed his brow.

"His name is Akeem," she whispered.

But her body had nothing left to give. The pain took over again, and her arms weakened. Her eyes dimmed, and then, stillness. The Magi stared in silence.

A mother dead. A father fallen. A prophecy hanging over them like a blade.

Shabazz was the first to speak. "We follow the second plan."

They wrapped Akeem in soft red cloth embroidered with symbols sewn in gold thread. He would not grow up in a palace. He would not know his father's last stand or his mother's last breath.

But one day, he would return.

And when that day came, he would fulfill the prophecy.

CHAPTER 1:

Whispers of the Lost Heir

The marble sculpture shattered against the wall, missing a trembling servant by inches.

Once part of a grand statue that had taken months to carve, it now lay in broken chunks on the floor. Muovu—once a general, now self-declared king—had destroyed it in a single, furious moment.

The servant didn't move. None of them did. Even a breath too loud could be fatal.

Everyone remembered the last time someone called him "General." A servant had brought food and uttered the forbidden word. Later, the tray returned, soaked in blood, the man's head resting on top. No one had dared say it again.

Muovu hadn't merely taken the throne; he'd seized it. And the word 'coup' had disappeared from palace mouths. That too had become dangerous. His anger had only grown over the years. So as restlessness. The man who once planned each step like a master tactician now moved like a fire out of control.

"I said," Muovu snarled, turning to the men seated before him, "repeat what they said about me!"

He had descended from the throne in fury, and now, standing before his council — the six men who called themselves his advisors — he was looking for someone to blame.

The man who had spoken earlier cleared his throat. "My king," he murmured carefully, eyes lowered, "it's nothing of substance. The people speak without understanding. They're ants beneath a lion. Feed them gold, and they still grumble. They aren't worth your concern."

Muovu stepped closer.

"But they are talking," he growled. "I've done more for them than anyone else. I pulled them out of the hands of a power-hungry royal family. I gave them a new order. I saved them!"

He slammed both fists on the table, and several men flinched. Only the speaker dared meet his gaze briefly.

"What more do they want?" Muovu spat. "Do they wish to sit on the throne themselves? Do they think they can oppose me?"

No one answered.

"I should remind them," he hissed. "Remind them what I am."

The air shifted. Even the guards along the walls stood straighter. Everyone remembered the last time Muovu "reminded" the people: seven days without food, borders sealed.

By the eighth day, they were on their knees. On the ninth, he opened the gates and flooded the streets with grain. They called him merciful as they ate with trembling hands. It was always the same. Terror, followed by false generosity.

Over twenty-five years, Muovu's rule had carved deep into the bones of the land.

"That would be good," said the first speaker cautiously, "but if we do that, we risk our standing with our supporters. They'll see us as weak. We have to show you're still in control. Let the people talk. Let them think they're free. Our real focus should be the Alkeic stones."

It was a bold suggestion, especially since the whispers among the people were growing hotter. But it wasn't as important as the stones.

Muovu's gaze sharpened. "And the boy?"

The room froze. No one answered. The wrong word would end in blood. But silence could be worse.

His breath deepened. And then, Muovu swept his arms across the obsidian table. Scrolls, maps, and glass shattered against the floor.

"How is it," he snarled, "that none of you can find one boy?"

But the boy was no longer a child. He was now a man, born around the time of Muovu's "restoration of order." And still, not a trace.

The council had searched everywhere, from bloodlines to royal sympathizers. Some claimed the Magi had hidden him. Others suspected Malaika's sister, who left before the fall. Every lead had vanished into thin air. It was as if the boy had never existed.

The second speaker, thin and sweating, mustered what little courage he had.

"We've followed every trail," he murmured. "It's possible he died. Or... the prophecy was false —"

"You read the prophecy wrong?"

Muovu struck like lightning. One second, the man was standing; the next, he dangled by the throat, Muovu's fist locked tight.

Red and gold light flared around Muovu's arm — his power sparking to life. The man's feet kicked helplessly, his brown face turning a deeper shade with each second.

"I've spent twenty-five years," Muovu growled, "chasing a ghost?"

The others stood at once, but none moved forward.

The first speaker raised his hands. "My king, please. He meant no insult. We only want to ease your burden. Let us help you."

Muovu didn't blink. Then, without a word, he hurled the man across the chamber. His body hit the stone wall with a thud. The others flinched, but Muovu's eyes never left them.

The man continued. "W-we're only saying it might not mean now. These prophecies can be unclear. It said the royal family would rule again, but look at us. It's been twenty-five years, and nothing has changed. Maybe fate still favors us."

Muovu stepped forward, watching the others shrink in fear. He liked it.

Back when he was just the general, these same men had kept their distance. They worshipped Jabari, the soft-spoken dreamer who couldn't lead an army if his life depended on it. It had been Muovu who built the military and who held the kingdom's spine together. But when he proposed an alliance with a global superpower, Jabari refused. All because of the Alkeic stones.

Yes, the stones had power. But Muovu had offered real transformation from trade to military support and even to international recognition. However, Jabari and his queen lacked vision. So Muovu planned.

But someone warned Jabari.

Muovu was summoned and questioned. But the king still trusted him then. So, he waited. Two years later, just as the queen announced her pregnancy, Muovu struck again, not out of hate, but necessity. He had wanted them out of power temporarily. After the dust settled, maybe something could have been arranged.

But Jabari had grown sharper and had spies to tail him. So, Muovu acted first. There was no other option.

Now, years later, the stones were still missing, likely hidden by the Magi or maybe by Jabari before his death. The thought unsettled Muovu as deeply as the scar that marked his own face. Each morning, when he stood before the mirror in his chamber, he traced that old wound—a line running from the bridge of his nose to the edge of his chin. It had been Jabari who gave him that scar on that fateful night. A permanent reminder of his failure.

He had been trained from birth to see every angle, yet somehow this blind spot remained.

Just like the secret passage in the royal bedchamber. When they raided the room, they found guards still inside, fighting to the death to keep anyone from reaching it. None surrendered. None spoke.

Muovu had lost it that day.

He slaughtered the guards himself, his power erupting, lighting the chamber with streams of red and gold. He couldn't let a blind spot get a hold of him.

He ruled Alkebulan now. The thought of losing it all to a boy boiled his blood. There would be no truce. No mercy.

"I want that boy found," he murmured, looming over a trembling councilor. "I don't care how.

That insect will not take my throne. Do you understand? Use every means to find him and the Magi. I want them found, dead or alive."

What he didn't say — what he wouldn't admit — was that the prophecy still haunted him.

It never said when the boy would rise. Only that he would. If it had foretold a distant future, Muovu could have died in peace. But Malaika had been pregnant the night of the coup.

It could be now. Or soon.

He also didn't believe the Magi disappeared. They were far too cunning to vanish without cause. Which meant they were preparing, probably training the boy.

He barked more orders. "I want eyes in every district. Spies on every street. Track any Magi sighting and report immediately."

The Magi held knowledge he never had, ancient truths about the relics, the land, and the old kingdom's secrets. They shared it only with the royal bloodline. And now, they were passing it to the child.

Rumors had surfaced of their appearances: three old men in the mountains, a silver-robed woman guiding a boy, and a child with emerald eyes whispering to birds. Lies, maybe—but lies had teeth.

If he could find the Magi, he would have the Alkeic stones. And also, the boy.

Time was slipping. The deal couldn't proceed without the stones. They were his last leverage. Without them, he had nothing.

And 'nothing' was not an option.

***

Atlanta

The room shimmered with golden runes, like breath on a glass. They hung in the air, visible only to the three who had put them there, not just in the room, but around the house, guarding it.

In the center of the room lay a young man, half-covered by a blanket, one arm flung over his head. He slept deeply, unaware of the three figures watching from the window.

"Twenty-five years," Shabazz said quietly. "Time moves faster among the unknowing." He stared at Akeem with the intensity of someone who had done all the calculations and found the outcome troubling.

Kwame tapped his staff twice against the ground. "Time moves no faster than a drumbeat," he murmured. "It's the dancer who forgets he's moving."

"Well," Shabazz replied, "this dancer forgot long ago. We've watched him for years, and still... nothing."

"Maybe it's not his time," Amani said from a floating chair, arms draped lazily along the back. He tossed a glowing fruit in one hand, catching it without looking. "Poor boy won't know if he's chosen or just breaking out."

Shabazz shot him a look. "This is not a joke."

"Neither is eczema," Amani muttered, then gave a smile. "But your point stands."

The others didn't laugh.

He sighed. "I've been too long among these people. I now understand their jokes."

Shabazz turned back, tuning the man out. For the first time in decades, he felt uncertain. He had studied every prophecy and mapped every star.

He thought the sign would come at thirteen when Akeem crossed into youth. Then again at eighteen. But twenty-five? That was the age when men began to forget the fire in their bones and began to settle.

He said, almost to himself, "Perhaps it's time to bring him home. We can force the awakening."

Amani stopped tossing the fruit. With a flick of his hand, it vanished. "You want to drag a grown man to a land he's never known, hand him a prophecy, and hope it doesn't crush him?" He raised an eyebrow. "We're Magi, not kidnappers."

Kwame's gaze never left the window. "We could bring him. By need, we have that right. But..." he tapped his staff once, "if we take him too soon, he may never trust us. And without his trust, he becomes a weapon pointed both ways."

Shabazz's tone hardened. "The prophecy doesn't care how he feels."

"But we should," Kwame replied. "Because if we don't... the prophecy might fulfill itself against us."

A heavy silence fell between them. Only the hum of the warded window and Akeem's quiet breathing remained.

Then Amani leaned forward, his grin disappearing. "It's happening again."

The others moved closer. Akeem had begun to twist in his sleep, brow furrowed, limbs jerking. His breath came quicker and a whimper escaped his throat.

"He's having a bad dream," Kwame said.

They watched, helpless. It wasn't the first time. The nightmares came often, and there was nothing they could do. The young man writhed as if under the weight of an invisible terror he could only see —

Then it happened.

A light flickered on Akeem's left arm, pulsing once and then again. Slowly, as if drawn by an unseen hand, it formed the shape they had been waiting for: a crescent moon above a circle.

For a long moment, none of them spoke. Then Shabazz exhaled.

"It's begun."

The heir had awakened.

CHAPTER 2:

The Mark and the Men

The creaming always came first.

Not one voice, but hundreds. Akeem stood in the middle of it all, surrounded by chaos he couldn't fully see but felt deep in his bones. Shadows flickered at the edges of his vision, and the stench of burning hung around him.

He tried to cover his ears, but his arms wouldn't move. His legs, too, were rooted in place. He was a prisoner and a spectator to a nightmare.

He hated this part.

Figures moved through the smoke. Some crawling, others falling. Someone shouted a name. Maybe his. Maybe not. The word slipped away before it reached meaning.

Then came the firelight.

But it wasn't fire. It was a strange purple glow that painted the sky. And then the voices. A man and a woman. Their words were often muffled, though one sentence sometimes cut through:

"Hide the child."

He never knew who the child was. But he knew what came next.

A blinding flash. A roar like thunder ripping the sky apart. The earth splitting beneath him —

Akeem jolted upright in bed with a gasp.

His room was dark and quiet, except for the hum of the AC. But sweat soaked the sheets, and he breathed deeply as if he'd run a mile. But it wasn't fear that woke him.

It was pain. He hissed, grabbing his left arm. It felt hot, as if there was a needle beneath the skin.

He flipped on the lamp, yellow light spilling over his arm.

Not a mark. More like a design of a crescent moon and a circle in perfect symmetry. He stared at it, unmoving. Then slowly reached for his phone. 3:02 AM.

He blinked. He rubbed at the mark, but it didn't fade.

"Must've scratched myself," he muttered, though he didn't believe it.

He lay back down, eyes wide open in the dark, staring at the ceiling until sleep dragged him under again.

***

The alarm blared at 7:00 AM.

Akeem woke up, heart pounding. He checked his arms, remembering the dream. The mark remained, clearer now in the morning light. This wasn't a dream.

Before he could think further, his bedroom door burst open.

"Happy birthday, Akeem!" His mother sang as she rushed in, followed by his father. They were still in their sleepwear. Between them, they carried a small cake glowing with a single candle.

For a moment, the dream faded. So did the pain. He smiled.

His parents were off-key and cheerful as they placed the cake on his nightstand. He sat up as they finished the song and blew out the flickering candle above the words "Happy 25th."

"How do you feel?" his mother asked, wrapping her arms around him as she sat on the bed.

At twenty-five, she still held him like he was five. But he didn't mind. He inhaled the scent of her favorite perfume, comfort blooming in his chest.

"Not much different," he murmured with a small grin. "But thank you. For all of this."

His father placed a hand on his shoulder. "We're proud of you, son. Happy birthday."

Then, turning to his wife, "Let's let him get ready. It's a big day."

And it was.

It wasn't just Akeem's 25th birthday. It was his graduation day too. A double celebration.

He finally pulled himself out of bed, going towards the bathroom. Flipping on the light, he blinked at his reflection.

Fresh from yesterday's cut, Akeem's high-top fade was still sharp, and his goatee was trimmed, thanks to his barber, who never rushed a job. Akeem respected that. If there was one thing he valued as much as his degree, it was presentation.

At 6'2", he had broad shoulders and brown skin that caught the light even at night. After stretching his arms loose, he slipped into his morning routine, freshened up, and headed to the kitchen.

As he walked in, the smell of fried plantains and spiced grits pulled him fully. His parents were already around the kitchen, probably conversing about work. Akeem watched them for a moment, smiling at the sight.

His height and build came from his father, a tall man with a beard he always took care of. Even in sweats, he looked like he was ready for roll call. His mother was a contrast: short curly locks and a wit sharp as a diamond—perfect for handling Atlanta's top clients at Maleek Law. And curvaceous in all the right areas, as Mr. Maleek would often say. Akeem would always cringe at those moments, pretending not to hear, while secretly grateful his parents still looked at each other that way.

"Sit down, birthday boy," she called, waving a spatula like a wand. "Before your father starts stealing off your plate."

Akeem chuckled. "Say less. I'm just here for the blessings."

He took his seat as she placed a plate in front of him—grits, scrambled eggs, sausage, toast, and fried plantains. Sweet and savory, just how he liked it.

He took a bite and exhaled. "Ma… this is magic. This is healing."

His father sipped his coffee, chuckling. "Careful. Say that too loud and she'll load you up with seconds before you can blink."

Akeem grinned, lifting his fork for another bite and then paused. His wrist had brushed the mark. The dream came back to him without warning.

"I had another dream this morning."

His mother turned first. "Like the others? Did you take your sleeping pills?"

She had kept those pills close since the nightmares began when he was young. They had helped sometimes. But not always. More often than not, he would wake up screaming, disoriented, trying to run from terrors no one else could see. He'd stopped relying on them years ago, only taking them to keep her from worrying. But last night, he had taken one.

"Yeah," he murmured quietly. "Still came anyway."

His father frowned. "It's probably stress. You've been pushing hard for finals. Maybe your mind's just unloading."

He meant well. As the owner of Alkemy Jewelers, Atlanta's most exquisite and exclusive precious African stone jewelry studio, burdened with orders, long hours and deadlines, his father knew something about pressure. But today, for once, he was home, and Akeem was grateful.

Still, he wasn't sure they understood.

"But it felt real." His brows furrowed as he tried to remember bits of the dream. "It felt like I was there—"

His mother crossed the room and placed her hands gently on his shoulders. He turned toward her.

"We've talked about this, Akeem," she murmured softly. "Nothing is wrong with you. Remember, the doctor ran every test, and he murmured the same thing. It's probably just stress from school." She paused. "That's why, after your graduation… your father and I booked you a full spa experience at Mara Oasis Retreat."

Akeem blinked, surprised. He had heard of Mara Oasis, a spa in the hills north of the city. Exclusive and way outside his usual budget. He'd never seriously considered going. Now, his parents had paid for it.

"Wow," he murmured, breaking into a grin. "Thank you, guys. This is… a lot."

He couldn't help wondering how much it had cost. He knew they could afford it—especially with his mother handling high-profile clients at the family's law firm—but he also knew they didn't spend carelessly. He had been saving, too, stashing money aside for a future apartment. Moving out had been on his mind more and more lately, but not today.

Today, they were here for him.

His father smiled. "Anything for you, son. Now eat up We're hitting the road soon, and we won't be late. Not on my watch."

Luther College was a solid two-hour drive away. The ceremony didn't start until 10 a.m., but Mr. Maleek lived by a code: early is on time, and on time is late. Akeem had heard it a hundred times growing up, and now, it was part of him too.

After breakfast, his parents disappeared to get ready while Akeem returned to his room. He changed into his dress clothes—navy slacks, a white shirt, and a burgundy tie that made his brown skin glow. Then, he draped his cap and stole over one arm.

His own car, a black sedan, waited in the driveway, but they'd be taking his father's SUV instead. His mom insisted they ride together, and besides, the birthday gathering she was "definitely not throwing" would bring them all back home tonight.

By the time they arrived on Luther's campus, the grounds were full of graduates in caps and gowns strolling around, posing for photos, and… a lot of excited screaming and hugging.

Akeem stepped out of the car and drew in a deep breath. He'd done it.

Years of late nights, quiet sacrifices, missed holidays, and focus had led here. A PhD in Computer Programming and Cybersecurity from one of the most respected HBCUs in the country. Luther had shaped him, and now it was releasing him into something greater.

And today wasn't just an ending. It was the beginning.

"Ayeee, look who finally showed up!" A voice called out behind him.

He turned, seeing his crew. Jelani, always the loudest, grinning with his cap tilted slightly to the side. Omari, more reserved, offered a nod. And Sade, wearing a colorful Ankara gown, threw her arms wide as she walked over.

They all hugged, teasing and laughing amongst themselves. Then he saw her.

Zaria.

She stood a few feet away, her black-and-white gown hugging her frame. She turned, and her lips, painted a deep red, parted into a smile. For a second, everything around him went quiet. Butterflies swirled in his stomach, that feeling he hadn't felt since high school. He offered a small smile. She nodded and then looked away.

"Akeem and Zaria under the tree, K-I—"

"Don't," he cut in, shooting Sade a look.

Jelani laughed. "Seriously, though, man, when are you going to tell her? It's been what? Years?"

He wasn't wrong.

Since that very first group meeting—back when Akeem sat across from the quiet girl with bright eyes and a bold stare—he'd been hooked. But he never made a move. First, because she was dating someone. And later, because the timing never felt right.

Now she was single. And he still wasn't ready.

"I don't know, man," Akeem muttered. "Let's just focus on graduation."

Sade stepped forward with a sly grin. "I can get her to come to your birthday party. We talk sometimes."

He gave a half-hearted shake of his head. "No, no... that's not necessary."

"Leave it to me," she murmured, already strutting in Zaria's direction.

Before Akeem could stop her, the loudspeaker crackled to life, calling graduates and guests to the main hall. The crowd shifted, moving as one toward the auditorium.

The ceremony dragged on for a while. The dean spoke, and then the alumni board president, followed by two city officials. Akeem sat mid-row, going through congratulatory texts on his phone. Occasionally, he looked up, his eyes drifting left to Zaria's row. She glanced back once and offered him another smile, just enough to think that Sade's plan might've actually worked.

Then came the awards.

Akeem sat up straighter as they called his name as the Top Graduating Scholar.

A burst of applause followed as he rose to his feet. As he accepted the award, he focused on his parents, who beamed at him with pride, and he smiled back. This was what all the sacrifices had led to.

When the ceremony ended, the crowd spilled back onto the campus lawns. There were hugs, photos, food trucks, and flying graduation caps. His parents were off mingling with the other parents. For a moment, Akeem stood alone, soaking it all in.

Then he saw them. Right across the field.

Three men stood beneath the tree like statues. The one in the center was tall, with dark skin and a beard so white and long enough to tuck into a belt. His robes were layered with a purple cloak that swept the ground, and a golden turban crowned his head. Behind half-moon spectacles, his eyes gleamed—deep brown shot through with gold.

At his side stood another, just as tall, his garments adorned with accessories. The last was shorter, but no less striking, draped in white garments. Akeem turned around, saw people occupied, and then turned back to them. They were still staring.

Then, they started moving forward, and he moved a step back but paused, not wanting to fall into someone behind him. They finally reached him, and in one fluid motion, they placed their right hands on their chests and bowed to him. Akeem's mouth opened. And then, the tallest one in the middle stepped forward.

In his hands, he held a small wooden box, carved with symbols. The man extended it toward him. without a word. Akeem hesitated, but something in him reached for it.

He opened it. Inside was a necklace of glimmering gold, strung with black and purple stones. There was a locket, and on it was the shape of a sun. In its center were words in an elegant script that, somehow, impossibly, Akeem could read:

"For the heir of Alkebulan."

He looked up, a question in his throat, but the men were gone. Vanished as if they were never there. He hadn't even heard the retreating footsteps.

The only evidence was the box, still warm in his hand.

***

Later that evening, as music thumped softly through the apartment walls, Akeem stood in front of his bedroom mirror adjusting his shirt. He had showered, changed, and tried his best to shake the strange moment from his mind. The box now rested in his desk drawer, wrapped in a T-shirt, too unsettling to look at but too powerful to ignore.

His parents hadn't noticed a thing. By the time he remembered to say something, they were already wrapped up in the celebration. He was just lacing up his sneakers when he heard a sound, like someone shouting. He paused. Maybe his friends had arrived early. Maybe Sade had actually convinced Zaria to show up.

Curious, he opened the door and stepped into the hallway. The living room lights glowed softly ahead. He rounded the corner and froze. His friends weren't there.

Instead, his parents stood near the front door and facing them were the three men from earlier. Still dressed in those indigo robes.

But this time, they smiled.

The one in the middle, holding onto a staff with an orb on it, stepped forward. His voice was deep as he spoke, "Betu, Akeem."

Akeem's breath caught in his throat. Everything inside him stilled, like the moment before a storm broke.

CHAPTER 3:

Truth Revealed

For a long moment, no one spoke. Akeem stared at the three strangers, mind racing. Had they followed him from the ceremony? Were they creditors? That made no sense. His family lacked nothing, and his parents didn't seem the type to owe dangerous people anything. But nothing explained how they knew his name.

"H-how do you know my name?" he asked, voice tight.

The shortest of the three, standing to the left of the tall one, answered with a smile. "We know everything about you. We are the Magi, and I'm Amani." He gestured to the tall man. "This is Shabazz, the Wise One. And that's Kwame. It's good to finally see you, Akeem. You're taller than we expected."

Kwame stepped forward. "It's time to leave. Get ready."

Akeem blinked. "Leave? I don't know any of you. How did you even get in here?"

His mother turned sharply. "You've seen them before?"

Still watching the strangers, he nodded. "At the ceremony. They gave me—" He stopped, regretting his decision.

"They gave you what?" his mother demanded.

"A box." He sighed. "I wanted to return it, but they were gone."

"We couldn't stay," Shabazz said. "Especially not when we were heading here."

Akeem frowned. "But why? What do you want?"

The tall man turned to his parents, then back to him. "I assumed you've told him?"

Akeem looked to his parents, usually composed, now standing pale and still, avoiding his gaze. It unnerved him. Giants in their fields, reduced to silence by three strangers dressed weirdly in the middle of summer. His party was an hour away, and the last thing he needed was friends walking in on whatever this was.

"I think you've got the wrong house." Akeem stepped forward, holding onto the door. "Whatever this is, it needs to stop. Please leave."

The men's smiles vanished. Shabazz's gaze narrowed at his parents.

"You didn't tell him?"

"Tell me what?" Akeem snapped.

"You're the heir of—"

"No!" his mother shouted, stepping between them. "Not today. Must you come here now, of all days?"

Shabazz's expression didn't change. "We told you we would return."

"It's his twenty-fifth birthday!" she cried. "You waited all these years, and now you want to ruin everything?"

Akeem's voice cut through them. "What are you all talking about?"

Silence fell.

Shabazz turned toward him. "We waited because the time wasn't right. But the sign has come." He stepped closer. "It's time for you to fulfill the prophecy."

His voice lowered into a whisper. "What… prophecy?"

The men's mouths fell open in shock. Akeem's father finally turned to him.

"Son, go to your room. We'll discuss—"

"No!" The staff struck the floor, silencing even the music Akeem hadn't even noticed until it went silent. Everyone flinched except the three strangers. "Enough of this aimless talk," Shabazz said, stepping forward. "It's time we sat."

"We have a party—" Akeem's mother began.

"Cancel it," he murmured, entering without another glance. "We have much to discuss."

***

The living room had never felt so full. Usually, it was always quiet, as Akeem was often at school and his parents at work, and even when home, they stayed in separate rooms unless sharing a meal or meeting. Now, it held too many eyes.

Two brown couches faced each other. Akeem and his mother sat on one, across from Amani and Kwame. His father took the chair at the end. Shabazz remained standing, staff in hand.

"You told him nothing of his lineage?" he asked.

Akeem's father exhaled. "We thought we could wait until he was older."

"Well, he's grown now. What kept you?"

"And tell him what?" His mother snapped. "That he's heir to a kingdom he's never seen, and three strange men would one day arrive to take him away?"

"Yes," Shabazz said, unmoved.

Amani offered a faint smile. "You could've left out the 'strange' part. You know we have good intentions."

Her voice trembled as she spoke, "You expect him to face the same man who murdered his parents. You call that good intention?"

Akeem's world tilted. He hadn't said a word, choosing instead to listen. But now, at her last sentence, something shattered.

"Killed my parents?" He gave a strained laugh. "But... you're my parents."

Silence. Amani and Kwame gave him solemn glances; Shabazz's face remained unreadable. His father stared at the floor. His mother's eyes were suddenly brimming with tears.

Something was wrong.

She looked up. "You're our son, Akeem," she murmured, her voice soft. "But your real parents—"

"Wait!" He jumped to his feet, suddenly towering over the room. Their eyes rose with him. "This is a joke. It has to be." He turned to the three men. "And you—you're actors, right? Some birthday prank? Did Sade put you up to this?" He laughed and clapped. "You got me. Seriously. I fell for it."

No one joined him.

The laughter faded into silence. He backed toward the wall, breath shallow. His hand brushed a photo frame—one of him as a baby, cradled in his mother's arms. He picked it up, held it out like proof.

"See? This is me! If I weren't your child, how—how is this real?"

"Because," Shabazz began, "on the day you were born, you were brought—"

"I'll tell him," Akeem's mother interrupted, wiping her face. She faced him directly, her voice now clear. "Akeem, I need you to listen. I was born into the royal family of Alkebulan—"

"We don't have much time," Shabazz interjected.

She lifted a hand, her eyes hard. "Give me a moment. I'll be brief."

He said nothing. She continued.

"I had an older sister who was heir to the throne, and since I was a princess, I didn't have many responsibilities, but I felt discontent. I wanted to see the world beyond the palace gates. I wasn't allowed, but I had my ways." She glanced at her husband, and they exchanged a smile. Then she turned back to Akeem. "On one of my secret rendezvous, I met him out there, and it was a funny situation. He, too, was of Alkebulan, though his family had left long ago. I'd met many men before, but this one… I knew he would stay.

"Romance wasn't forbidden, but as royalty, I couldn't marry anyone. Still, I fought for it. I pleaded with my parents, and when that failed, it was my sister — Malaika, your real mother — who stood by me. She understood what freedom meant to me, even though it broke her heart."

Her voice trembled. "Back then, I told myself I left because I wanted to breathe beyond the crown. But the truth is that I was jealous. Laika carried the kingdom on her back while I resented the attention always on her. Now I know… she must have been lonely, and I left her to bear it alone."

She paused, swallowed hard, then met Akeem's eyes again.

"So, when the Magi came, carrying a child and told us of the coup—of how your parents were gone—I didn't wait to take you, especially since we've been trying to conceive for years. That night, when I held you in my arms, I saw more than a burden. I saw a second chance."

The picture frame slipped from Akeem's hands and hit the floor with a soft thud. His legs felt unsteady.

"So, I'm not your son?" His voice cracked. "Why didn't you tell me? I would've understood."

His father finally spoke. "We wanted you to live free."

"But that is my life!" Akeem burst out. He didn't know what stung more—the lies or the theft of a history that was his by right. "You should've told me."

"The prophecy is cruel," his mother said, rising. "It asks a boy to kill the man who took everything from him. That's no child's burden."

"He is not a child," Shabazz said, and the room stilled. "The more you embrace the truth, the clearer it will become. The prophecy has waited for this moment."

Akeem stood in silence, the word prophecy ringing in his ears. They had spoken around it, but never of it.

"What is this prophecy?"

"Now you ask the question that matters." Shabazz began to pace slowly. "Years after your parents were crowned, a prophecy came that one close to the crown would bring ruin. Your father, noble as he was, trusted Muovu — his friend, also the general — and didn't heed our advice of casting him out. By the time he fully realized it, it was too late." He stopped, eyes meeting Akeem's. "Your parents fled, but Muovu was faster. He took your father's life. For your mother, her eyes closed finally after your birth, and we had a duty to keep you safe. It's why we hid you in the only place Muovu's reach could not yet touch. But even then, the prophecy spoke further."

His voice became lower.

"'The fruit of the royal family shall disrupt the enabler of chaos and bear the burden that is to come, if he allows it.' That fruit... is you."

Akeem shook his head. "It could mean anything. Maybe it's not me. Maybe it's someone else. Don't I have cousins?"

Amani rose. "We searched, but every sign pointed to you. The mark, the dreams—"

"How do you know about the dreams?"

"Because we are the Magi. We see more than what the eyes reveal. We uphold the pillars of Alkebulan, and now, we are here to guide you back to your path."

His voice wavered. "Wait. Tell me about the dreams first."

Amani nodded slightly, and for a moment, the room seemed to darken. And Akeem listened as the man described the dreams in detail: the chaos, the running shadows, the screams, the purple flash of light. He had told his parents all these, but he was unsure they knew the real deal like Amani did. It unsettled him. It was as though Amani had also been inside the dreams.

As if reading his mind, Kwame spoke as he rose up. "We are not the cause of your dreams, Akeem. But we understand the realm where you wander when you sleep."

It still felt unreal. "No. This is all just… coincidence. Weird magic talk."

Kwame raised an eyebrow. "Was it a coincidence when lightning struck the swing set, and yet the fire didn't touch you?"

Akeem froze.

"Or when the river rose in seconds on the school trip and everyone panicked, but you stepped into it and the waters stilled?"

His breath caught in his throat. He had buried those childhood memories and labeled them strange.

Shabazz stepped forward. "And the mark on your arm, show it."

Akeem lifted his left arm reluctantly. His mother gasped as she rushed to his side, fingers trembling as she touched the symbol. His father leaned closer, eyes wide.

"Nya na Zua," Shabazz murmured. "That is no ordinary mark. The moon and the sun are the royal sigil of Alkebulan. No surviving kin bears it, for Muovu wiped them out one by one. Only those far beyond his reach still live. And of them… none bore the sign. The ancestors have spoken. You carry the balance we have waited for."

"I d-don't understand. Then, why didn't they come for me?"

Kwame answered. "Because we shielded this place. So long as you remained here, you were a shadow to him. But the moment the mark surfaced…"

He didn't need to finish the sentence. Akeem could feel it.

"Now, we must leave—"

"Wait," Shabazz interrupted. "The necklace we gave you has a locket on it. There's a message inside. Bring it."

With a glance at his parents, who nodded at him, Akeem dashed to his room, retrieved the box, and returned. At Shabazz's instruction, he pressed the center with his thumb.

"Only your DNA can open it," he murmured.

The box clicked open. Inside were two familiar faces—his parents, it seemed. Then a glow burst from the locket, and a hologram bloomed above: two life-sized figures resembling the ones in the locket formed in the air.

The man spoke first.

"Akeem... if you're hearing this, then you've grown into the man we always hoped you'd become. Your mother and I are proud of you, son. The Magi are family, and you can trust them with your life. Be compassionate towards them, for they love you with all their hearts. And if this message has reached you now, then Muovu has broken the oaths. He has turned his hand against the throne and against our people. But you, Akeem, you are Alkebulan's hope. Walk in strength and know that no matter where you go… the blood of kings beats in your chest. I love you, son. Never doubt that."

Queen Malaika spoke next in a soft voice. "My sweet Akeem… oh, how I wish I could hold you now. I can only imagine the man you've become. You've always been destined for more, my love. Even when you were in my womb, I knew you were born with a purpose. And though I am not there to guide your steps, I am with you. And one thing you should know, you were never abandoned. You were hidden until the right moment, which is now.

"The kingdom needs you. But more than that, your people need hope. And no matter what happens… I love you."

The projection dimmed. Silence fell. Akeem sank into the couch, shaken. He had heard his true parents' voices. Was he trapped in a divine puzzle he never agreed to play?

"I hope you understand now," Shabazz said quietly.

"I… I need time. I need to process this."

"We don't have it."

Akeem looked around, disoriented. Everything felt unreal.

"Muovu has hunted you since the moment you were born," Shabazz continued. "Now that the mark has awakened, he will come."

"They are already here."

It came from Amani, who held up a device that pulsed red. Akeem hadn't seen him draw it from his robe, and he could have sworn those garments had no pockets at all.

Shabazz went pale for the first time.

"We need to leave now."

CHAPTER 4:

Hidden Palace

Akeem wasn't new to the strange.

Once, when he was young, while walking home, a group of high school bullies had cornered him for his money. They outnumbered him and closed in, delivering blows to his body and then, in a flash, an unseen force hurled them backward. He'd run, too stunned to question it, and later chalked it up to adrenaline or luck.

The other occurrences had been the ones Kwame mentioned. The ones he figured were just coincidences. Now, as he stood on the edge of something he didn't understand, those moments returned in full force.

He turned to his parents. "Let's go together —"

"They can't come," Shabazz said. "It must be you alone."

"No way." Akeem's eyes widened. "What if Muovu comes for them?"

"His eyes are on you, not them," Shabazz said, stepping closer. "The longer we wait, the more we risk your safety."

"No—" Akeem began, but his mother's voice stopped him. He turned. His parents stood before him, their eyes heavy with sadness. "Please," Akeem whispered. "Don't say it. We are going together."

"We can't," his mother said. "The prophecy was clear. This path belongs to you alone."

"That doesn't mean you have to stay behind—"

"We would only hold you back," his father said, stepping forward.

Akeem's heart pounded. "I'm not ready for this."

His mother cradled his face in her hands. "None of us are. But we know you, Akeem. We raised you to stand in truth. Now, walk in it." She pressed a kiss to his forehead. "You're not just our son. You're Alkebulan's heir."

Tears slipped down his face. He wasn't sure when he'd started crying. She embraced him, and his father joined in too. After a few moments of sniffing, they separated. Then, his mother gestured for him to wait and returned with a large shawl—red, trimmed in gold.

"This wrapped around you the night they brought you to us. I saved it for this moment."

He raised it to his face, inhaling a scent both foreign and warm.

Behind them, Shabazz cleared his throat. "It's time."

Akeem nodded, though nothing within him felt ready. He bent to pick up the fallen picture frame from earlier, but Kwame stopped him.

"Let it go," he murmured quietly.

His anger flared. "So, I'm just meant to leave everything I've ever known and become king of a place I've never seen?"

The silence that followed said everything.

Akeem looked around the room — the life he had built — and then turned to his mother one last time.

"Go," she murmured. "Let them keep you safe."

Something in her certainty stilled him. She had known these men once. She trusted them. And because she did, he found the strength to do the same. He pulled both parents into one final embrace, then stepped away.

Outside, the evening was unnaturally still. Not even wind. As they turned the corner, Akeem's mouth opened. Floating just above the street was a massive, spiral-shaped vessel. A ladder extended downward, waiting. It looked like something that didn't belong in this world.

He stared. "How is this even here? Won't someone see it?"

Kwame gave a small smile. "One, it's our ship. Two, it's shielded. No one sees what isn't meant to be seen."

Akeem turned to his parents, still standing at the doorway, their silhouettes framed by the light. The weight of their sadness nearly dragged him back. He wanted to stay, but something inside had already shifted.

He took a deep breath and stepped forward. With every rung he climbed, he was shedding one life and entering another. By the time he looked back, he was inside, the door closing behind him. His parents became small figures swallowed by distance, and within seconds, the vessel rose.

The inside was large and warm, its architecture carved with swirling symbols. A great screen hovered above the floor, glowing with a map. On it, unfamiliar lands shimmered; one, he guessed, was Alkebulan. The three Magi moved toward the display. Amani turned, glancing at Akeem and beckoning. Akeem joined him.

"You have questions," Amani said. "Many of them."

"We're going to Alkebulan?"

"Yes... and no."

He frowned. "I thought that was the whole point."

"All in time," Amani said. "But first, you must understand your origin. Your bloodline traces back to Queen Malaika and King Jabari, and far before them, a dynasty of rulers who shaped Alkebulan into what it is until Muovu ruined it."

Akeem folded his arms. "If that's true, why haven't I heard of this place? Sounds like some tiny, forgotten nation tucked away."

Shabazz finally spoke. "Because we chose silence, but Muovu wants to tear the veil and drag us into something we may never escape. That's why we came for you."

"How am I supposed to defeat someone like that?" His gaze swept around them. "You three seem powerful. Why not just stop him your-selves?"

They exchanged glances before Kwame an-swered.

"We tried. But fate has its chosen vessel—you, not us. Our duty is not to fight for you, but to pre-pare you."

Akeem laughed bitterly. "And if I die? Is that part of fate, too?"

No one spoke.

He backed away, retreating to a seat far from the glowing screen. He was grateful they didn't fol-low. The silence gave space for the dread swell-ing in his chest.

How long would he need to train? How could he face a man who had spent twenty-five years gathering power? This wasn't a mission; it was a sentence.

"Am I ever going to return home?" he muttered, barely above a whisper.

They heard it.

Shabazz approached slowly, stopping in front of him. His gaze was calm.

"You've lived a beautiful life," Shabazz said, his voice low with something like grief. "Your parents' sacrifice made that possible. You may see us as thieves, tearing you from the world you knew, but that isn't our aim. We came only to return you to who you truly are. The prophecy waited until you were ready. Now, ready or not, it calls."

Akeem's voice rose. "What if I don't want this? What if this isn't my path?"

Shabazz's gaze fell. "It is the glory of God to conceal a matter," he murmured softly, "but the glory of kings is to search it out."

"What does that even mean?"

But the man had already turned away, returning to the others, who turned silent. No matter how often Akeem pressed them, they gave no answers. He began to question their motives, despite his mother's words. How could he trust those who had taken him from the only love he had ever known?

They ignored every mention of his parents, as though he was expected to forget the last twenty-five years of his life and embrace destiny like it was owed to him. He wanted to scream, to ask who had the right to declare such a future.

It was only when Amani finally spoke that the silence broke.

"We're almost home."

The screen shifted, displaying a live view. Akeem stood, bracing for his first sight of Alkebulan, but saw only forest.

"Where's the city?" Suspicion crept into his voice.

"We cannot enter openly. Muovu controls the palace and watches the skies. We've built a hidden fortress here, beneath the forest's veil. This is where we've waited for you."

A jagged rock formation appeared ahead, but as they neared, its mouth opened like it was yawning. The ship descended. The sky outside darkened.

"We're here," Shabazz said.

There was no welcoming committee. Just silence and swift movement through unfamiliar corridors. By the time Akeem was led to a chamber—spacious and warm—his legs ached.

He collapsed onto the bed, heavy with exhaustion. He would have loved to explore, but there was no time. Sleep came quickly, dragging him into its depthless sea—

Snap.

He bolted upright. The window was open, moonlight coming through. He got out of bed, approaching cautiously. The forest beyond was silent, but he had heard it. Like a foot snapping a branch.

Nothing was there. Still, the chill lingered.

He returned to the bed, trying to convince himself it was nothing. And then, like a weight too heavy to resist, sleep embraced him once more.

CHAPTER 5:

Lessons Begin

keem awoke to the sound of singing. At first, it floated through the fog of sleep like a distant river until it sharpened and got clearer. The voice wasn't his mother's, as her songs were mostly off-rhythm, but this one was different. It was sweeter and more melodic.

He pushed himself up slowly, his body still heavy with sleep, and blinked at the figure before him. A girl, no, a young woman, stood at the edge of the room, wearing two thickly braided ponytails and a sleeveless, dashiki-style top tucked into wide-legged black trousers. Bronze armbands circled her upper arms, etched with symbols he was beginning to get familiar with. A leather belt hugged her waist, and from it peeked the hilt of a dagger.

She placed a bowl on the wooden table near his bed, then turned. Her eyes widened, and her hands shot to her mouth.

"Oh, by the gods!"

Akeem blinked. The phrase sounded like an ancient version of a curse word. "Um... hi?"

She squeaked something close to a greeting, then dropped suddenly to her knees, bowing so low that it caught him completely off-guard.

"I offer my sincerest apologies, my lord! I thought you were still resting! I just wanted to prepare everything for your waking, but I didn't realize—"

"It's fine, really," Akeem said quickly, trying to calm her, but she was already deep into her performance.

"This humble servant seeks only your mercy! But if you want me whipped—"

Akeem recoiled. "Whipped? No! Why would you even say something like that?"

She looked up, blinking rapidly, as though confused. "I thought you were angry…"

"I'm not," he murmured, shaking his head. "Even if I were, that doesn't justify violence. I wouldn't whip anyone. Ever."

She sprang upright with a swiftness that startled him once again. "Of course not, Your Grace! I was only… seeking your forgiveness." Her speech had a rehearsed rhythm, as though reciting from memory.

Akeem exhaled, rubbing his face. He wasn't even fully awake and already felt like he'd run a mental marathon.

"It's alright," he muttered. "And... your singing was actually pretty good."

Her expression brightened immediately. "Thank you! I learned it from my mother."

"She taught you well," he replied with a tired smile, swinging his legs over the side of the bed, only to be intercepted.

Before his feet could meet the floor, she darted forward, unrolling a thick mat beneath him. The speed and swiftness were so perfect that Akeem froze for a moment.

"Um, what for?"

She looked up proudly. "Your Grace's feet must never touch ordinary ground. You are of the royal bloodline. The earth should honor you, not humble you."

"That's a bit much," he muttered, stunned. "Really... I can handle it."

She straightened her back and folded her hands. "Forgive me, but your comfort is my calling. I am Nala, your personal guard and royal aide. My duty is to serve your every need."

Akeem blinked. The way she murmured it made him feel more like a museum artifact than a living person. It felt strange.

"That's... uh, kind of intense. Do I get a say in that?"

She didn't answer his question. Instead, she smiled again and launched into an explanation, proudly sharing how the palace guards had conducted a series of trials to find the most suitable attendant for the heir. Though she'd been nearly rejected by the chief guard for talking too much, she'd won through determination. Now, she was here to serve, and nothing thrilled her more than fulfilling that role.

Akeem barely kept up, nodding as she called him "Your Grace" and "my lord," as if trying to test which one fit better.

"Okay, Nala. I get it," he murmured eventually, though he didn't, not really. She wasn't the person he needed answers from. "How old are you, anyway?"

"I'm eighteen."

He studied her for a moment. "Really? You look younger, like fifteen."

She grinned. "You should see my friends. Twice my size, half my brains."

"That... sounds interesting," he murmured, turning away to finally examine the room he'd woken up in.

114

It was grand in a way that made his childhood home feel like a storage shed. The ceiling shimmered with light patterns, and the walls were painted blue with faint gold carvings. He had been noticing the gold too much. On his right, Nala was already opening doors, revealing a bathroom and a walk-in wardrobe filled with clothes and footwear he'd never owned before or dared to try on before. Everything seemed to glitter. It was as though they got everything in the mall they shopped at.

On the left was a desk with a computer. He rose, walking toward it, hoping to connect with someone back home.

"No social media," Nala said, her voice now low. She was behind him again, holding up two shirts—one white, one blue. "They don't want you distracted."

His eyebrows rose, though he no longer felt surprised. "Wow."

She gave a faint smile and then asked instead, "Blue or white?"

He looked at the garments, then at her waiting face.

"Just pick anything. I trust you."

She gave a slight nod and busied herself, while Akeem turned to the window again, thoughts drifting to the sound he'd heard the night before. It had startled him then, but now it seemed like nothing.

Drawn by the sunlight, he stepped closer to the window. The forest outside seemed alive, with the rhythm of birdsong and rustling branches. He could spot a few vibrant-feathered birds flitting through the green, and it felt like a hidden paradise. And yet, for all its beauty, it wasn't home. His parents were still far away.

If he truly meant to understand what was happening, he'd have to meet Shabazz and start figuring things out. Fortunately, Nala had already laid out his clothes—the blue shirt and fitted pants, paired with leather slides "to preserve the sneakers for special days," she had explained. It suited him, as if his world hadn't changed.

A knock, then a voice: "Akeem?"

He turned to find Shabazz standing in the doorway, staff in hand. Without waiting for an invitation, the elder stepped inside, his eyes roaming briefly over the space before settling on Akeem.

"You've adapted quickly to Nala's touch," he murmured. "She was proud to serve you this morning."

"I'm not sure I need her," Akeem replied, folding his arms. "I've always done things myself."

Shabazz offered a small smile. "That may be, but she's not just a helper. Think of her as a shield."

"I just don't think I want someone following me wherever I go."

"Alright then. I'll tell her to give you some space."

Akeem sighed and then gestured toward the computer. "And what about that? There's no internet to reach my parents or friends? What are they thinking right now?"

Shabazz didn't even glance at the device. "Your parents have been assured of your safety, and they trust us. We will send word to them later, though I'm afraid you will not be permitted direct contact. Not yet. The road to reclaiming

Alkebulan comes with sacrifices. Let us ensure they are not in vain."

The words settled heavily on Akeem's shoulders. He sat down slowly on the edge of the bed, rubbing his hands together. "So, what's the next step, then?"

"You begin training today. Martial arts, philosophy, and etiquette."

"Etiquette?" Akeem raised an eyebrow. "Like, which spoon to use first?"

"Among other things," Shabazz replied. "You're a royal, Akeem. You must learn to walk as one, speak as one, and command as one. Amani and Kwame will introduce you to our history and customs. Others will follow."

Akeem exhaled slowly. "It's a lot."

"Only if you give little to it. Now go eat. You'll need your strength."

The old man left him to his thoughts. Soon after, Nala returned and led him to the next room, where a table awaited him, covered with dishes of warm food that he couldn't name but smelled good. As he ate, Nala chattered beside him, sharing idle gossip and exaggerated tales of how everyone had waited so long for the heir's return. The weight of expectation pressed on him with each bite.

By the time he finished, he needed air.

Sensing his discomfort, Nala suggested a walk. She guided him through halls and rooms like the infirmary if he got sick and the library, which he only peeked at, until they reached the outside. He took a long breath and stared around him, startled by how the architecture blended into the landscape. The building they exited was disguised in stone and plants, as if part of the foliage itself.

Then, they followed a gravel path through the forest. For once, Nala was quiet, which he appreciated. The air was filled with the sounds of chittering creatures, rustling leaves, and in the distance, a swishing sound.

Akeem paused, ears sharpening.

Another swish.

He turned toward the sound, curiosity pulling him off the path. He didn't hear Nala's protest and turned to see that she had disappeared. Another swish. He returned to the sound, following the noise through a clearing until he came upon a circular open space, filled with sand. At the center, a woman dressed like Nala was moving. Or dancing. He wasn't sure of the exact word.

She wielded a curved blade, her body in sync with the strike of the weapon. Every step she took stirred up dust, and surrounding her were streaks of light. Akeem stepped forward, entranced. He had never seen anything like it.

At first, he tried to find a logical cause behind the lights. Were they from fireflies? But no, he had seen fireflies before, and these were no insects. The light moved as she moved, not behind or around her, but with her. As if anticipating her moves. And it wasn't only the lights that held him spellbound.

It was her. There was something about her that commanded his sight to stay on her. It was the fluidity of her motion, as though her body already knew the steps to a choreography passed down through generations.

Just as he took a step forward, trying to get a better view of her face, he heard someone call his name. Her focus didn't break, and not wanting to disturb her, he stepped back slowly. He turned to find Nala approaching.

"Magi Amani is asking for you," she murmured with a slight bow, "so you can begin your history lesson."

He opened his mouth to ask about the woman in the sand, but he paused. There would be time for questions later. For now, he would follow where the path led. He nodded, and she guided him down another pathway that curved back toward the building.

After several turns, they reached the library he hadn't initially given a lot of thought to. The moment he stepped inside, he stopped, awe spreading through him like fire.

It was beautiful.

The domed ceiling soared above, and beneath it stood endless shelves filled with books of all sizes, stacked so perfectly. He didn't think there were just hundreds — there were thousands. And in the middle was a circular desk under a wide skylight where the sun streamed in. Amani sat on a chair, reading a book, which he put down as he looked at him.

"Come," the man said with a smile, gesturing to the empty chair across from him, "take a seat."

Akeem obeyed, his gaze still roving across the sea of books. On the table before him were three books, their covers aged except for one, which looked relatively new.

"These books," Akeem said, pointing to one, "they're not in English. What language is this?"

"That," Amani replied, "is Alkala, the tongue of this land."

"Alkala," Akeem said, trying out the word. "Was that what you three said when you arrived at my house?"

He nodded. "Betu means 'Hello.' It's a customary greeting here." He then spoke a long sentence in Alkala—at least Akeem thought it was a sentence, perhaps more—and ended it with another smile.

Akeem blinked and gave a sheepish shrug. "I didn't understand a word."

Amani chuckled softly. "That's expected. Your parents must have chosen to withhold it from you, likely to allow you a more 'ordinary' life. But it is a language you must eventually learn. I will not ask you to master it overnight, but it's better to learn some phrases." He pointed to the books on the table. "For now, start with this." Then he touched the new one. "Read this first."

Akeem stared at the stack. "What... what are they about?"

"Your history," Amani said, folding his hands atop the desk. "The rise and fall of your line. The enemies we have faced. The bloodlines that shaped you. You must know the foundation upon which you now stand if you are to walk forward."

Akeem hesitated. "I was never really good at history."

Amani tilted his head, as if amused by the comment. "Ah, but this is not some distant empire of dead men and forgotten wars. This," he murmured, tapping the top book, "is your blood. You will find yourself in these pages."

"You don't expect me to finish all of these to-night, do you?"

The elder raised one brow, picked up his book, and began reading. The conversation was over.

Left with no other choice, Akeem pulled the top book closer. Its cover bore an embossed emblem—two lions encircling a sun with a crescent moon above it—and the title was etched in both English and Alkala. He opened to the first page.

The Story of the 250th Royal Family: Malaika and Jabari.

His parents. He straightened in his chair, no longer feeling reluctant but alive with curiosity.

Whatever he thought he knew, it began here.

CHAPTER 6:

Guarded Intentions

keem spent the entire day reading. So engrossed was he that he missed lunch, only rising for dinner because Nala practically dragged him to the table. It struck him as ironic. Back in Atlanta, he had gone out of his way to avoid history books, only skimming through them only to keep his grades from tanking. But this book was different.

It wasn't just a historical account. It felt personal. This was the story of people who had lived and ruled and they were his blood. And Akeem, for the first time in his life, felt connected to his history.

He didn't sleep early that night either. Even when the stars and moon appeared in the sky, his eyes were still locked on the pages. Nala, who knew some of the tales, had offered to fill in the gaps, but he asked her to hold off. He wanted to hear it all from the source first. When she saw the way he clutched the book, she quietly brought him a notebook and a pen, which he appreciated.

He began jotting things down.

One of the first things that struck him was Alkebulan's adherence to monarchy, not just as a tradition, but as a spiritual and political thing. It was a sovereign nation built on continuity. And even though Shabazz had mentioned that Alkebulan chose to stay small, Akeem found it almost unbelievable. Given the level of technology he'd glimpsed—like the vessel—it was hard to imagine this place had remained hidden from the modern world.

The more he read, the more questions he had.

He noted the many changes in the royal line. While most rulers had been succeeded by their direct children, there were instances where the throne passed to siblings or nephews when no heirs were born. The kingdom also had its own share of strife and political issues. It made Alkebulan feel more like a living place.

And then there was the story of his parents.

His mother, Malaika, was not only the rightful queen by blood but had also passed several tests that proved her courage, wisdom, and connection to the ancestral spirits. That last part intrigued Akeem the most. He circled the section, marking it for his next conversation with Amani.

His father, Jabari, had a humbler origin. Born to a farmer, he knew a lot about plants. Akeem paused there, imagining a man who might've helped him back in middle school when he nearly failed a science project on botany. His adoptive father had been too busy, and the man definitely didn't have a green thumb. Akeem had ended up winging it with a cactus he bought from the corner store.

But Jabari seemed like he would've known what to do. That realization hit him strangely hard.

Jabari had once trained in the borderlands to become part of the Royal Guard, known not just for its elite combat skills but for its loyalty to the Crown. To be chosen was an honor, as they got access within the palace and the pay was good too. Yet it came at a price. Service meant surrendering your life to the safety of another. That part unsettled Akeem, who couldn't help but think of Nala.

Among Jabari's fellow trainees had been Muovu. Both warriors had endured the same trials and emerged at the top of their cohort, earning entrance into the Sentinel Guard, a position for those charged with the royal family's direct protection.

Jabari had been assigned to Princess Malaika, though at the time she paid little heed to the guards surrounding her. Her younger sister, however, was a different story, as she was quite restless.

His and Malaika's interactions weren't a lot until she made a journey into the city where she got ambushed by a group opposed to the monarchy. Jabari, without hesitation, threw himself between her and a blade, taking the wound to his chest.

That moment changed everything.

While he recovered, Malaika visited him often, ensuring his recovery. It became the beginning of something deeper. Still, their bond didn't blossom immediately into romance. According to the book, it began with sparring, both with blades

133

and with words. Once Jabari regained his strength, the princess, well-trained in swordplay, challenged him to practice.

Malaika admired his honesty and Jabari, in turn, admired her strength and the way she let her guard down in his presence. Over time, they fell in love, which defied custom.

Alkebulan's royal code forbade royalty from marrying below their station, but the two of them challenged the very law. It also helped that they had earned the people's favor and, after coronation, even united divided tribes through diplomacy and combat challenges.

Akeem paused, struck by it all.

Just before dawn, he reached the final chapter and closed the book slowly, exhaling as if he had been holding his breath for hours. There was much to process. Among their many accomplishments, the tale of Alkebulan's resistance against foreign domination stood with him. For generations, foreign powers sent veiled threats. But in the early days of his parents' reign, one nation had made its intentions plain. It came not with proposals but with armies.

Jabari and Malaika led the defense themselves. With no foreign aid but strategy, the Alkebulans refused to be conquered. The counteroffensive was swift and victorious.

Yet peace didn't last as the prophecy emerged and with it, Muovu's betrayal.

Akeem remained seated at his desk, eyes fixed on the window. There was still so much he didn't know but for now, he loved that he now carried a clearer image of his parents.

He slipped into bed, letting sleep pull him under.

***

Morning came wrapped in Nala's relentless commentary sprinkled with unsolicited gossip and reminders to stretch, breathe, and drink more water. Akeem tolerated it, mostly because he wasn't ready for silence.

After breakfast, he asked Nala for space. Not in anger, just the need to breathe. She didn't take it personally, flashing a grin before skipping off.

He wandered the palace grounds, feet tracing the gravel path into the forest until he heard it. The sound of a blade slicing air. He followed until he reached a safe distance.

The woman of yesterday moved, the sword catching glints of light as it swept and turned. There was something more to it—maybe technological—woven into the metal of the blade. He would have to ask.

But for now, he simply watched.

From a distance, crouched behind a flowering bush, he studied the way her form curved with each swing. For a few moments, he watched and then she suddenly paused.

Her head snapped in his direction. Akeem ducked fast, heart thumping against his ribs. He waited until the swishing resumed. Only then did he leave.

***

"The Africa you know is the version edited for comfort."

Amani's voice resounded in the library as Akeem sat across from him, glancing at a book he hadn't yet opened. He'd expected more stories about his parents, but the teacher had other intentions.

"Um," Akeem began cautiously, "I wouldn't say I know that much. Just what my parents told me and stuff I looked up. But... why do you say that?"

"The Western media and the global North have painted a distorted picture of Africa. They portray it as a land of constant strife, poverty, and corruption — images that fit their narrative of superiority and control. But the truth is far more complex."

Amani rose and picked up a wooden staff, pointing it toward a wide scroll pinned to the wall, which showed a sketched view of a map.

"This is Gao," he murmured, tapping the parchment. "Capital of the Songhai Empire. Before Oxford laid its first stone, Gao's streets were lit with lanterns, having lots of scholars, ports and healers."

Akeem squinted. "I think we covered Songhai in class. Just a bit. Mostly how it fell apart. They had no central government; there was tribal conflict; and they had a weak military. That sort of thing."

Amani turned to him. "That is the story told by strangers holding our pen." Akeem shifted in his seat. "You were taught to see war, disease, and famine. A continent waiting to be saved. But what you weren't told is that we had great cities from Timbuktu to Meroë to Zimbabwe." He let the staff fall softly to his side. "We built flood-resistant towers before modern engineering had a name. We didn't just live; we understood."

That felt very poetic and he would have mentioned it but Akeem frowned, remembering something.

"But we never learned that. Like… we only ever heard about Egypt. And even then, it was like it wasn't really 'Africa.'"

Amani chuckled dryly. "Egypt is spoken of like it floated above the continent. But the same soil runs from Giza to the Congo. They want you to marvel at pyramids but forget Nubia, the queens who reigned, the bronze work, and the science. You know of Newton's apple, but not of Imhotep's scalpel."

"Wait. Who?"

"Imhotep. He was an architect, priest, and healer. The first recorded doctor in human history." Amani paced now. "And our blacksmiths were not ordinary. They listened to the hum of metal and forged more than blades. It was like they communicated with the spirits too."

"Okay," Akeem drawled out slowly. "That's… not what I got from school. I mean, we had African History Week once. We mostly watched 'Roots.'"

Amani looked at him with something like sympathy. "I watched that once and inasmuch as it explained some things, it doesn't tell the major truth. Our past didn't begin with chains. It began with crowns. Not all history is lost, Akeem, and that's what you'll learn too."

There was a silence. Akeem stared down at the book in front of him, his fingertips brushing a symbol he didn't yet understand.

"So… what do I do with all this?" he finally asked. "How is it going to help me fight Muovu? I mean, he's powerful. I'm just… a guy from Atlanta."

Amani's lips parted to respond, but the moment was interrupted by the creaking of the door behind them.

Akeem turned, expecting Nala with another cup of tea or a servant bearing books, but instead, it was Shabazz. And beside him stood someone who made Akeem's breath still.

It was her. The woman from the training yard.

Akeem had seen beautiful Black women before on campus, in passing, but none like the vision before him now. She was taller than she had seemed at a distance, with a lean frame. Her black trousers rippled softly with each step, as if moving like water. Her sleeveless tunic bore symbols and on her arm was an armband etched with symbols. At her waist hung a long, curved blade in a sheath. Her skin was the color of clay and her braided black hair was adorned with bone beads that clinked faintly.

When their gazes met, Akeem felt as if she looked straight into his soul, which left him strangely exposed.

Shabazz stepped forward and gestured between them. "Akeem, this is Imani, your royal chief guard. She will oversee your martial instruction."

Akeem swallowed. He hadn't expected to see her again so soon, and certainly not like this.

"I… saw you earlier," he managed, gesturing faintly. "You were training in the forest."

Imani didn't respond. Her face remained still, as if carved from the statues he saw around. For a moment, he wondered if she'd even heard him.

Shabazz spoke into the silence. "She has trained from girlhood by the best warriors across the kingdoms and now, she will train you. Three sessions each week. You will begin with Engolo, the dance of the body. Then you will learn Laamb, where balance and spirit meet. Finally, she will instruct you in Tahtib, a discipline of rhythm and stillness."

Akeem tried to hold all this in his head, but he was still anchored to the presence of the woman before him. Her silence did not bother him but intrigued him.

"I understand," he murmured finally, turning back to Shabazz.

Shabazz nodded once, then turned to go. Imani followed, silently and Akeem's eyes followed her as if pulled by a thread. Amani cleared his throat and Akeem turned quickly, his ears becoming hot. He hadn't meant to stare.

But there was something in him that stirred—he didn't know what to name it.

***

Later that evening, as he left the library, Akeem found Nala waiting outside the door with a look that said she'd been holding in conversation all day.

He then decided to ask what had been on his mind since morning. "So... Imani," he began, slowing his pace so she could catch up beside him.

"Yeah, she's the chief now. The youngest one we've had in a while."

"Chief as in... head of the royal guard?"

Nala nodded so enthusiastically her hoop earrings danced against her cheeks. "She was already one of the highest-ranked fighters before the last chief retired due to illness. They didn't even hesitate and appointed her quickly. Nobody questioned it either. She's that good."

Akeem took a moment to absorb that. "She seems... serious."

"She's more than that," Nala said, her voice slipping into something more reverent. "She's disciplined. She's led missions into the desert and once fought off six bandits alone at one time."

"So, was her family in the guard too?"

"Oh, not just in it," Nala beamed. "Her grandparents were part of the Queen's escort. Her mother too. She served your mother directly, long before she became queen. It's in her blood. You could say the chief was raised in the palace but trained in the wild."

Akeem let out a low whistle. "So, she's basically a legacy."

"A prodigy," Nala corrected, placing both hands on her hips. "She was wrestling palace guards twice her size at age ten. You'll be fine with her. In fact, you're in the best hands you'll ever have. She doesn't say much, but she sees everything."

Akeem had more questions. He wanted to know what drove Imani, what she believed, and a lot of 'whats.' But for now, he held them back, content with what little he'd learned.

Everyone trusted her and that meant he would too. And he wouldn't earn her respect by birth-right or title. He would have to prove himself and he would.

CHAPTER 7:

Unready

keem wished he had asked Nala more about Imani.

Now, standing in the center of the open-air training yard, he felt every inch of that silence like a stone pressed against his chest. The early morning wind curled around him, tugging at the edges of his tunic, longer than Nala's but cut from the same cloth meant for practice. It was the right fit, and though it was supposed to be comfortable, he felt anything but.

The yard stretched wide, its edges lined with weapon racks that held everything from practice blades carved of wood to steel spears and modern training gear laced with faint blue circuits. Every piece looked polished, as if waiting for battle. The ground was covered with deep green mats, each one bearing the golden insignia of Alkebulan: an eagle in full wingspan.

Along the edges stood carved wooden benches, each one adorned with markings, made for trainers or warriors catching their breath.

Akeem doubted he'd be using them anytime soon. Not with the way Imani was watching him. She moved in slow, silent circles around him, like a panther measuring its prey. She hadn't said much since they stepped onto the mat. She didn't have to. Her eyes said it all.

Akeem swallowed again. That made it what, the tenth time in five minutes? Maybe more.

He was not used to this. He had never felt so scrutinized, and not even in a humiliating way. It was more like being measured. As if she were assessing his spirit. What was there, and more importantly, what was not?

And the worst part was that he wasn't sure he liked what she saw.

His height had always made people back home pause and gave him a presence even when he didn't speak. But none of that meant anything here. Here, Imani was only slightly shorter than him, her eyes level with his brow, but she carried herself with such confidence that she might as well have been looming over him.

Funnily, her face was small-featured yet her confidence was strong. He'd noticed the wrinkle on her nose when she was displeased; she'd done it the first time they met. And now, once again, her nose wrinkled as she stopped pacing and exhaled through her nose.

"Your posture is poor," she murmured, tone flat. "And you don't seem to be taking this seriously."

Akeem straightened so fast it nearly looked like he'd been struck.

Not because she was wrong—he had been slouching slightly, unsure of what to expect—but because of her voice. It wasn't soft, and it wasn't melodic like Nala's, but it had a texture to it. It wasn't the kind of voice that begged for attention; it claimed it. It was the voice that called you awake at dawn and dared you not to rise. He didn't have the words for it yet, but whatever it was, he liked it.

"Sorry if it looked that way. I mean, it is my first time being out here," he murmured, with a grin. Maybe she'd smile too.

She didn't.

So, he let his smile fade. "Sorry," he added quickly. Then, trying to change the conversation, he coughed lightly and said, "So, um… Shabazz said you'd be teaching me martial arts. Is this, like… karate? Or something like that? 'Cause I saw you earlier—"

"It's not karate," she interrupted. "You won't be doing any of that."

He blinked. "Oh. I thought that was kinda the point."

Imani's gaze didn't soften. "Melanic energy. Alkeic stones. Kemistry. These are the foundations of your training. Not karate. Not boxing. And certainly not whatever you've been fed through colonial entertainment."

Akeem frowned. "'Melanic'? What's that? I've never heard these terms before."

Her head tilted slightly, just enough to let him know she was trying not to sigh. "Every child of

Alkebulan knows them. But I suppose I must understand that you were raised away."

It wasn't unkindness but there was something beneath her words. It felt more like disappointment that wasn't directed at him alone but at something larger.

She stepped back. "But today, we begin with understanding."

Akeem exhaled, glancing toward the rising sun. "So… no fighting? This feels more like a classroom under the sun."

She didn't blink. "Without knowledge, your fists are useless. Melanic energy is the root. Everything else—your stance, your strikes, your breath—grows from it."

He raised an eyebrow. "Is that like… chi? You know, anime chakra vibes?"

Imani stared at him long enough that he started to regret asking.

"No. This is not a cartoon. Melanic energy lives in all things, but in us, with more melanin, it hums deeper. It is power."

"So… like… Black people have superpowers?"

"In a way," Imani replied, but her voice didn't lighten. If anything, it deepened. "But not the way you're imagining. This is not about shooting lasers from your hands or flying through clouds. Melanin is a key to the divine."

She stepped closer. "In Alkebulan, when melanic energy is awakened, the individual becomes something else entirely. They become healers, warriors, and seers. They are the builders of balance."

While Akeem tried processing her words, she reached for the small pouch attached to her waist. She then pulled forth a smooth stone that pulsed with a bluish light, as if it had a heartbeat.

"These are Alkeic stones. They do not just store energy, but they echo it. Each one is attuned to its bearer's spirit."

Akeem narrowed his eyes. "Like a USB drive for magic?"

Imani's expression tightened, though her head dipped slightly. "Crude, but not entirely wrong."

He grinned. "Cool. So, how does it work?"

"You awaken it," she replied, returning the stone to her pouch. "And that awakening comes through learning Kemistry."

Akeem blinked. "Wait—chemistry? I barely passed that class."

"No." Her voice sharpened. "Kemistry with a K. It is the sacred art of balance and transformation. Its origins lie in the temples of ancient Kemet, before the tongue of conquest named our knowledge."

She turned slightly, facing the ground, then knelt and drew a triangle into the sand with her finger.

"This," she murmured, "is the foundation. Kemistry stands on three pillars."

Akeem leaned closer, watching her trace each point of the triangle.

"At the apex," she murmured, tapping the top, "is Kemetic knowledge. We study the Maat codes, which unlock patterns of energy within the body and the realm beyond."

"Like… runes?"

"Yes, but older than them." Her finger moved to the lower left point. "Here are the Solomonic scrolls. Ancient writings encoded with seals and numerology. Through them, we learn the power of Alkealpha Gemetria. They teach us to bend melanic energy where we shield, bind, heal, sever curses, and banish restless spirits."

"Wait… for real? Like Ghostbusters?"

Her eyes narrowed. "This is not play."

"Right, sorry," he muttered, rubbing the back of his neck.

Imani's hand moved to the final corner of the triangle. "And here," she murmured, "is Gemetria, the mathematics of the cosmos. Through it, we map melanic energy across convergence lines. There are sacred points across the land where power breathes most clearly. Nzambi's Eye. The Spiral Path and the Flame Wells."

Akeem stared at her, slightly slack-jawed. "You sound like a walking wiki page."

She rose, brushing her hands clean. "That place doesn't always tell the truth. This is the real deal."

He nodded slowly. "So, all this has been here this whole time and nobody back home talks about it?"

"They talk," Imani said, her voice colder now. "But not in your schools. They buried your language in other people's alphabets and told you it was lost."

Akeem went quiet for a moment and then sighed. "What happens next?"

"Now," she murmured, kneeling once more across from him, "we begin the Ankh Transfer. The first step in waking your melanin."

He blinked. "Awaken it how?"

She dipped her head slightly. "The Ankh is more than a symbol. It's also a conduit. Through it, we pass energy. In rare moments," her voice dropped, "it can even be used to transfer one's very life to another. But that is a final act, meant only for times when the balance must be restored at great cost."

Akeem's brows drew together. "Wait, like giving up your life for someone else?"

"Yes. But that is not your path today. Don't let your thoughts wander there." She shifted. "This is the beginning. What we do now is about learning. The rest will come."

Akeem half-laughed, thinking she might be joking but her expression didn't move.

"Oh. You're serious. How long does it take?"

"As long as it needs."

"Awesome," he muttered. "Guess I'm not going to lunch, then."

Imani ignored the comment and folded her legs beneath her, spine straight, palms facing upward. She became still.

"Your body," she murmured, "is an instrument. The Ankh does not force energy; it draws it in, like the lungs draw air, and redistributes it through the heart center. Your breathing must align with the pulse of the earth. You will listen, feel, and direct."

Akeem blinked. "And… I'm just supposed to feel that happening?"

"You do not force it," she murmured again, this time softly. "Your body already knows it. You have simply never listened."

He tried to sit like her, awkwardly crossing his legs and straightening his back. His breath came too fast at first, so he tried to slow it. In. Out. He looked over. Imani was still. Not even her eyelids twitched.

He shut his eyes. Nothing happened.

His thoughts immediately betrayed him.

I wonder if Imani ever laughs. She's probably judging me right now. I can't feel any melanin thingy. What if I make a weird noise accidentally? Did I forget to drink water?

His brow furrowed.

"Stop thinking," Imani said, eyes still closed.

"How do you even — ?" He opened one eye.

"Your breathing is erratic. Start over."

He sighed and tried again. This time, he focused on his breath. In. Out. Breathe.

But as the silence stretched around him, a question crawled out from the back of his thoughts: Why didn't Mom ever talk about this? If, as Imani had said, every child of Alkebulan knew it, then why had no one spoken of it back home? Then again… she had done yoga nearly every morning. Maybe that was her way.

Akeem's breath caught in his throat as his concentration broke. He exhaled heavily. "This isn't working."

"Again," Imani said without opening her eyes.

He clenched his jaw, nodded to himself, and gave it two more tries. The quiet wasn't helping; it only gave the noise in his mind more room to breathe. He squirmed.

By the fourth attempt, he was already frustrated, and he dropped his hands to his thighs with a groan. "Man, this is hard. My mind just won't shut up."

At last, Imani opened her eyes. Her eyes lit with a mix of judgment and patience. "You fight your mind like it is your enemy, but you need to know that thoughts are not intruders. If you stop chasing them, they will sit beside you."

Akeem let out a dry laugh, half embarrassed. "Yeah, well… My mind's a noisy neighborhood. I've never been good at this. This seems a bit boring."

"It's not. You simply don't yet understand the power of stillness."

He nodded. "Alright, well, I might suck at meditation, but I do know taekwondo. I've been training since I was nine. So, you know… maybe I can show my moves? I gotta learn how to fight too, right?"

She didn't answer immediately, but her posture shifted subtly. Then, wordlessly, she rose to her feet. She unclasped the sword at her hip and placed it on the ground. She rolled her shoulders once.

Akeem bounced lightly on the balls of his feet, grinning. "Alright then. Let's go."

He moved first, stepping into a front kick meant more to test her reactions than to cause real harm. But she didn't block and simply swayed. His next jab met only air as she stepped aside. He struck again, faster this time. She caught his wrist and her body turned.

And suddenly the sky was above him. Akeem landed flat on his back, breath knocked from his lungs.

He groaned, blinking. "Okay. Ow. What the hell was that?"

"Engolo," she replied coolly. "One of the old styles." She made no move to help him up. She simply waited.

Akeem sat up, rubbing his shoulder, wincing. "No mercy, huh?"

"You asked to spar."

He looked up at her, wondering if he'd over-stepped. Her face remained unreadable. He was about to make a joke to break the silence when something stirred in his memory.

"Hey, uh… something weird," he murmured, brushing dirt off his arm. "The night I first got here, I heard a sound—"

"Where?"

"Oh, um, outside my window."

"You should have reported it immediately."

He blinked. "I didn't think it meant anything. I mean—I wasn't sure—"

"If it felt wrong," she murmured, her tone urgent, "then it did. Trust that."

"Alright, I will. Next time, I promise."

She bent to retrieve her sword, returning it to the sheath. "That's enough for today," she murmured, already turning away. "But I advise you to continue practicing the Ankh transfer. It will not meet you until you stop chasing it."

"Yeah," he murmured, rising and brushing off his pants. "I will. Promise."

She gave a nod, turning to leave, when he hesitated.

"Wait—before you go. Can I see the royal guards sometime?"

She turned. "Why?"

"Nala mentioned there's a group. I just thought it'd be cool to meet them. You know, see who's protecting the palace. Maybe even thank them."

"The Royal Guard is not for curiosity. They are sworn to protect you and it's best you focus on your own duties."

"I get that," Akeem said, lifting his hands a little. "I just thought… Knowing the people who are watching your back can't be a bad thing, right?"

Imani's eyes flicked over him like a scan. Then, without another word, she gave a small bow of farewell. "Goodbye, my lord."

She turned and walked away.

Akeem exhaled, rubbing his palms together. That… went okay? He wasn't sure. It wasn't bad but she hadn't exactly invited him to tea either. Just as he was about to leave, he heard Nala's voice.

"You're still standing. That's a good sign."

She was approaching him, a grin tugging at her lips.

"Where've you been?" he asked.

"I'm always around. Besides, as much as I'm your protector, Your Grace, I'm also under orders not to smother you. Shabazz said so."

There was a playfulness in her voice, but Akeem winced a little at her words.

"I didn't mean to report you," he murmured quickly. "I just… didn't want someone hovering over me every second. That wasn't what I —"

"I know," she murmured, waving a hand. "That's why I gave you space today."

He smiled. "Alright, thank you."

They walked back to his room, where she gave him privacy and he freshened up. When done, he went to the library to go through the books Amani gave him. He didn't know how long he'd been reading when a knock rapped against the doorway.

He looked up, blinking from the page. Shabazz was behind, walking toward him.

"How was your training?" the elder asked.

Akeem sat up straighter, closing the book shut. He hesitated. He could tell the truth about how he failed the meditation. About how Imani flipped him like a leaf in the wind. But the words stuck in his throat.

170

"It was… fine," he murmured instead, forcing a nod.

Shabazz said nothing for a moment. He only looked at him.

That look. Why did everyone in this place do that? Imani, and even Nala, like they were all expecting him to suddenly become something.

Akeem shifted under the gaze, then added, "I mean… Imani introduced me to some concepts. Things I didn't really know. I'm… trying to get on with it."

Shabazz's features softened. He nodded slowly.

"Good. I believe in you."

Akeem blinked, unsure of what to say. "Thanks… I mean, really."

Shabazz stepped farther into the room, his hands clasped behind his back. "Tomorrow," he murmured, "there is something we must do. We will be going out."

"We?"

"Yes. You and I."

"Where are we going?"

The old man turned upward. "To the city."

Akeem's head snapped toward him. "The city?"

Shabazz looked back, the faintest smile touching the corner of his lips.

"There is much you have yet to see."

CHAPTER 8:

Among the People

Akeem sat at the table, his eyes fixed on the untouched toast and lukewarm cup of tea before him. He stirred the liquid absently, appetite now distant, while the morning sounds drifted through the air — soft voices in the corridor and the cry of distant birds. Yet for all the palace's splendor, he felt uneasy.

His thoughts circled the same questions: What sort of city had he inherited? Was it still the same place his parents had built, or had it become something darker?

Judging by what Shabazz had told him of Alkebulan, he feared it was the latter. But why take him into such a place now? Why risk capture at all, when his presence could upset all they had labored to protect?

He hadn't been able to ask the Magi those questions. Shabazz had simply left with a cryptic promise: "Your questions will be answered later." Akeem had scoffed at that. No way would he risk his life just so the old man could make a point.

He sighed heavily. He'd barely taken a sip when a quiet voice interrupted his thoughts.

"My lord, you've barely touched your meal."

He looked up, startled to see Nala standing there, brown eyes sharp and bright. "I'm not hungry," he muttered, pushing the cup aside.

Her brows furrowed. "Is there something troubling you, my lord?"

Akeem hesitated, unsure whether to tell her. Then, he realized he could go about it in another way. "Nala, can you tell me about the city? I'm stuck in here, yet I feel like a stranger in my own home. I need to understand what's happening beyond these gates."

Nala's eyes softened. "Of course, my lord, I'd be honored."

He gestured toward a seat, which she sank into. And then she took a breath.

"The city," she began, "is not what it was. My parents say they've never seen such fear, and they believe our ancestors didn't know it either. I was born after Muovu's uprising, so I never knew the city as it once was. But even I can feel how wrong it is to live under his rule."

Her voice trembled. "They call him the Oppressor. Anyone who dares utter that name is seized and dragged away to the palace. They never come back. Even during the day, his men patrol the roads, watching for the smallest sign of rebellion."

Akeem's breath caught. "How did you all come to be here?"

Nala leaned closer, her ponytails brushing the table's surface. "One night, two masked men took me from my home. They asked if I wished to be part of something that could bring down Muovu. I was terrified at first, but they treated me with respect. I told my parents, who no longer worked with the guards as they couldn't serve Muovu, and though they feared for me, they urged me to go. They hoped it would be my chance to help end the darkness. Many of us were gathered in the same way, and we've built trust with one another. Magi Shabazz says that if that trust breaks, then everything we've built here might crumble too."

Akeem's thoughts churned, but another question burned on his tongue. "You said the city was divided. Does that mean some people support Muovu?"

Her jaw tightened as bitterness flashed across her face. "It's complicated, my lord. Some have prospered under his rule, like those who helped him during the coup, who were rewarded. And not everyone loved the royal family; there were conspirators who were always there, always whispering against the throne. Muovu claimed to be the shield against rebels, but they don't realize that he is the rebel who shattered our peace."

Her voice dropped. "But it's not fair. Living in fear, knowing that one day you might be here and the next, gone. There's even a curfew. It's so hard."

Akeem's chest tightened. The weight on him increased. It was too much, and the worst part was that he was headed into that very place with no clear plan. What did Shabazz expect of him? To lead an uprising overnight?

"Is there anything else you need, my lord?" Nala's question brought him back.

He shook his head. "No… I was just curious." He rose, and then Nala reached to clear the dishes but paused, looking back at him. "My lord, if I may…"

"Yes?"

"I don't know what's going on in your mind, but I can only assume you're trying to understand it all. I just want to say — don't think it's your fault. None of us blame you."

He hadn't asked for her sympathy, but her words eased something in his chest. "Thank you, Nala."

She returned to her work, leaving him to his thoughts.

In the quiet, he drifted to his room. With no lesson scheduled, he had time to prepare for the journey, but the thought of reading felt hollow. People were waiting for him to stand against Muovu. But he hadn't even set foot in the city, and already he felt small.

A knock broke the silence, and he sat up from his bed. Shabazz stood at the door, Imani beside him. Akeem rose, startled to see her and momentarily forgetting his mission.

"What's going on?" he asked, eyes darting from Shabazz to Imani as they entered.

"She's joining us," Shabazz replied. "We can't enter the city without a guard, and who better than Imani?"

Akeem frowned. "What about Nala? She's my personal guard."

A shadow flickered across Imani's face, gone so quickly he wondered if he'd imagined it.

"If you'd rather, we can assign Nala," Imani said coolly.

He opened his mouth, but Shabazz spoke first. "Nala is fine, but Imani's knowledge is unmatched. I don't expect trouble, but caution is wise."

Akeem exhaled, feeling half-relieved and half-strange about Imani's presence. She didn't even seem fazed, only scanning the room like she was measuring him. Shabazz stepped forward, holding out a necklace — a glass pendant shaped like a horn, swirling with purple mist.

"What's that?"

"A talisman to hide your identity," Shabazz explained. "It will mask your voice and features enough to pass for an ordinary man. You look too much like your father, and we can't risk that."

"Wow. Will you two be wearing one as well?"

Shabazz nodded. "Muovu's men have eyes everywhere, and there's a proclamation to report anyone suspicious. We don't want to risk anything."

Akeem's brows lifted. "This feels like we are spies in a John Wick movie."

He'd expected a laugh, but Shabazz's face darkened instead. "This is serious. At no point should you remove that necklace. It's the only way we can slip you in and out of the city. Every step we take is watched, and even the smallest misstep could draw attention. Just don't stray from us."

He pressed the talisman into Akeem's hand, and he wore it, just as the others did. Immediately, something in his chest stirred like a ripple across still water. Akeem glanced at them—Shabazz looked younger, while Imani's gaze softened, her clothes shifting to a simple wrap. Her sword disappeared, but he was sure her blade was concealed somewhere.

"Good," Shabazz said. "Now, let's go."

They stepped out of the room and saw Nala waiting in the corridor. She didn't even look surprised and just gave a nod, as if she understood everything.

Outside, a vessel — smaller than the first one Akeem saw — stood.

As if hearing his silent question, Shabazz leaned in close to Akeem. "To avoid Muovu's patrols, we'll disembark a few meters from the city gates."

Akeem just nodded, unsure of what to feel. He boarded the vessel and sank into the seat, his hand on his chest, trying to quiet the pounding. The ride didn't take long. Within minutes, Shabazz stood and said, "We're here."

They stepped out into a forest, the air heavy with the scent of damp earth and flowers. Shabazz led them through the trees until they reached a clearing where the city walls loomed.

Shabazz turned to him. "Once again, we're only here to observe. We don't talk to anyone and don't draw attention. We're just another part of the crowd, understand?"

Akeem swallowed hard and nodded.

As they neared the gates, his chest tightened. There was a table near the entrance where two guards sat, checking tags. Around them, more guards lined the walls, their armor gleaming in the sun. Behind the table, an open gate beckoned to them. The whole place pulsed with tension.

A line of people had already formed, each one clutching a tag, waiting their turn to face the guards. As Akeem watched, a man was suddenly shoved out of line. He hit the ground with a thud that made Akeem flinch.

Shabazz whispered. "Some don't have proper tags. It's a risk every time they come in or out."

The guards barely glanced at them as they stepped forward. One took their tags and held them over a small device. It flared blue, a light that seemed to cut right through them before fading. The guard handed back the tags without a word.

As they walked on, Akeem whispered, "What was that light?"

Shabazz murmured back, "It's a scanner that verifies the tags. But we are safe because these aren't real."

As they moved deeper into the city, Akeem's stomach churned. The place was a dump. The air reeked of cow shit mixed with something rotten. He instinctively lifted his hand to cover his nose.

The houses were slapped together and made from mismatched scraps of wood and corrugated metal, some leaning like they might collapse at any moment. Smoke from small fires curled into the air, mixing with the stench and turning it all into a choking fog.

He saw a homeless man curled in a doorway, knees to his chest, staring blankly at the ground. Others sat on broken steps or on the ground itself. Frowns creased nearly every face, and their eyes flickered with suspicion as they passed.

He turned to Shabazz. "What happened here? This place—"

"It wasn't always like this," he murmured. "Once, this place thrived. The markets were alive, children ran through the streets, and there was laughter. Now…" He gestured to the broken walls and garbage piles, his face hardening. "Now it's survival." He turned to him. "Don't cover your nose. They're used to it here; don't show them you're not."

Akeem swallowed and nodded, trying to look unfazed. But inside, his heart pounded. The city felt like a war zone.

He also noticed guards at corners, watching the passersby. Now and then, one of them would slip from his spot to follow someone, stopping them to ask questions. None approached their group; it felt like Shabazz's magic was working.

Just as they passed a fruit vendor, a child ran toward them, stumbled, and fell. Akeem instinctively reached to help, but a shout came from behind. He turned to see a young woman rushing at him, looking panicked.

"Get your hands off my child!" she cried, snatching the child away and then disappearing into the crowd.

Akeem stared, stunned. "What was that about? I was just trying to help."

"She knows," Shabazz said. "Muovu has taught these people to fear even a helping hand. It makes them believe that any kindness comes with a price. People don't trust each other anymore."

"I still don't get it. Is this how it's supposed to be?"

Shabazz's gaze turned somber. "There's a word, Ubuntu. It means 'I am because we are.' You'll understand it better in time, but for now, just know that every man, woman, and child is bound to the next like a single note in a song."

Akeem looked around. "It doesn't feel like that now."

"No. Muovu has broken that harmony. He rules through fear and has turned neighbors into informants. The frequency of Ubuntu is shattered."

A chill ran down Akeem's spine. This was more serious than he thought. Just as they moved again, he noticed two guards who fixed their gaze on him. His skin went cold. They peeled away from the wall, heading straight for them. His heart leapt.

Then, from the corner of her mouth, Imani hissed, "Stay still."

Akeem froze.

The guards stopped inches away. One of them spat on the ground and barked, "Show me your tags."

Shabazz didn't flinch. He reached into his pouch and handed over the tags.

"What are your names?" the guard demanded.

Shabazz rattled off something in Alkala. Akeem only caught one word—"Betu"—before the guards exchanged a look and grunted. They moved on, but their eyes lingered a moment too long.

Akeem let out a slow breath and turned to Shabazz. "What did you say?"

Shabazz gave a tight smile. "Told them we'd just visited family. Said, Imani's my wife, and you're our son."

"Oh, okay."

He pointed to a nearby building. "Let's head over there. It's a bar where people go to talk. We might hear something useful."

Inside, the place felt familiar, like the dive bars back in Atlanta he'd snuck into at eighteen. They ordered drinks and found a table near a group of men hunched in whispered conversation.

"Keep your ears open," Shabazz murmured, "and you might learn something."

Akeem leaned in.

The men were discussing a friend who'd vanished after speaking out. One suggested revenge, but the others shook their heads. "If Muovu's men caught him just for talking, they'll catch us too," one muttered.

Then the talk shifted—worry about feeding their families and the struggle to survive under Muovu's rule. They couldn't leave without a reason, and even then, there was no guarantee they'd be allowed to go. It felt like Muovu wanted them to suffer.

One thing struck Akeem: none of them mentioned his name. He brought it up to Shabazz, who turned to Imani.

"The people don't really know you," she answered. "They know the idea of you, that you're alive and that one day you'll fulfill your purpose. But that's it. Out of sight, out of mind. Some still believe you'll come back, but years have passed, and nothing's changed. It's like you're a story they tell their children, not a hero they can reach. And tonight, this is just the tip of the iceberg. There's more he's done, and we have to take it back."

Akeem let the words sink in. He knew he needed time to process it all, but even then, he couldn't escape the weight of it.

A wave of nausea rose in his throat. His vision blurred. The walls seemed to close in. Without warning, he stumbled back, shoving past chairs and bodies, ignoring the startled voices around him. He barely made it outside before he doubled over, hands pressed to his mouth.

Nothing came up. Just a dry retch that left him gasping.

"Are you alright?" Imani asked, appearing beside him.

Akeem shook his head. "I — I just — please, I need to leave. I want to go home."

Imani's hand reached for his shoulder, but he flinched away, shoving himself upright. He didn't want to be touched. He turned and started walking away, not looking back. Didn't want to feel the weight of it pressing on his chest like a stone.

He just kept moving, as if he could outrun the truth.

CHAPTER 9:

Fractures

On the way back to the vessel, everything was quiet. As he entered inside, Akeem took a far seat, his head bowed, resting between his knees. Footsteps echoed, and he tensed, praying it wasn't Shabazz. But the voice that came was Imani's.

"Are you okay?" she asked.

He wanted to tell her no—that he was far from okay—and ask if she would be in his place. But they'd had that conversation before, and she'd just looked at him with that same unreadable expression that made him feel like a child trying to explain the sky to a hawk. So, he only shook his head.

She murmured nothing, but he felt her hovering nearby. He didn't look up, focusing instead on his breath, which felt uneven. The hum of the ship only deepened his unease. Finally, it settled with a shudder. They'd landed.

Akeem raised his head to find Shabazz and Imani staring at him. He didn't speak, just stepped off the vessel, pushing past them.

Nala stood at the building's entrance, a bright smile on her face. But as soon as she saw the look in Akeem's eyes, her smile faltered. Akeem walked past her without a word, the others trailing behind him. He didn't know where else to go, so he led them straight to the library.

He turned to Shabazz. "You told me we were going to the city. You said I'd see something waiting for me, but you didn't tell me it was this. People are suffering, Shabazz. I don't understand why I'm even here. Is it a punishment or a test?"

Shabazz watched him with that same look Akeem had come to despise — a calm gaze that made him feel like a child reciting a lesson.

"This is your prophecy," Shabazz began, but Akeem cut him off.

"No. Don't talk to me about prophecy." His voice shook. "Forget prophecy. Talk to me like a human being. Have you even looked at what's happening to me? Have you tried to understand?"

Before he could finish, Nala's voice rose gently, "Maybe the prince needs to rest. He's had a long day."

Akeem's chest burned. "No. I don't want to rest."
He turned his gaze on each of them, lingering on
Imani, whose expression was as hard to read as
the rest. "What do you all want from me? Why
am I learning all these things when people are
suffering? You say you can't even stand up to
Muovu yourselves, so why would you think I—
someone who's never lifted a sword—could do
it?" His voice was shaking now. "What can I do
with dusty books? Why should I care about the
stone of melanin or the chemistry of dust when
you can't even use your own technology to save
yourselves?"

For a moment, no one spoke. He clenched his
fists, staring down at the people who seemed to
hold every answer but refused to give him any.

Then Shabazz spoke, his voice calm. "Akeem, if
we could save ourselves, we would've done it a
long time ago. But this—" he gestured around
them "—this is bigger than any of us."

"You keep saying 'prophecy' like it's supposed to
fix everything."

"Forget the prophecy for a second. You're the
Prince of Alkebulan, and you have a duty to help
these people. That's why we brought you here to

train you. If we were as reckless as you think we are, we'd have thrown you into the fire already. But we didn't. We want you to be ready."

"Ready? Thanks for taking me from my home — the only home I've ever known — and dropping me into a world where I'm supposed to save people from someone you can't even stop. And now you want me to believe it's all about destiny. Does that even make sense to you?" He shook his head. "What if I'm not the right one? What if I'm just… an impostor?"

"You're not an impostor." Shabazz struck his staff against the ground, and the sharp crack made Akeem flinch. "We've looked at the prophecy every way we could. If you weren't the one, you wouldn't be standing here."

Suddenly, footsteps rushed in from the hallway. Amani and Kwame appeared at the door, with widened eyes. The latter glanced from Shabazz to Akeem and back again.

"Is there a problem?"

Imani crossed her arms. "Seems like the prince is terrified of stepping foot in the city, which — " she shrugged " — makes sense. But we're back at square one, and now he thinks the prophecy isn't about him."

Akeem shot her a glare, not liking her tone. "I didn't say that. I'm just saying… there's a lot on my mind. I don't want to be the one who lets everybody down."

Silence wrapped around them again. Akeem tried to steady his breathing, realizing what he'd been trying to say all along: the idea that he was supposed to defeat this monster felt impossible.

How could he defeat a man who'd been ruling with iron and fire for twenty-five years? He couldn't even defeat Imani in sparring. He wasn't weak, but every time he faced her, she was stronger. He'd never tell his friends back home that.

But before he could voice his fears, Shabazz spoke up in a soft voice. "Akeem, I apologize. But that visit to the city was necessary. You needed to see what's at stake. It's not just about you — it's about the people who've been waiting for their rightful king."

He paused, letting the words settle. "We've tried everything to stop Muovu, but every time, it comes back to you. You're our only hope, and I know that's a heavy burden to carry. But we are with you all the way."

Akeem looked at them, saw not just expectation but desperation in their eyes. It terrified him more than anything. He tried to swallow the panic that bubbled in his throat.

He took a shaky breath. "Fine, let me talk to my parents. I need to hear their voices."

Maybe that would calm him for a while.

"The necklace we gave you can connect you to them—"

"Not those," Akeem cut in sharply. "I mean, my parents, in Atlanta."

Shabazz's gaze softened, but his answer came quickly. "I'm sorry, Akeem. You can't have any direct contact—"

Akeem's anger flared. "You had me paraded through the city like some trophy, but you're telling me a call to my parents would put me in the spotlight? That's hypocrisy!" He turned to the others. "Can't you see this?"

Imani spoke up. "Akeem... the necklace you're wearing was the only thing that kept the guards from finding you. Even that wasn't a reliable shield."

Then, Amani stepped forward. "The plan was to allow you to see what's out there. You need to understand brokenness before you can heal."

Akeem barely heard them. Without a word, he turned, left, and tossed the necklace on a table by the door. He heard footsteps behind him and saw Nala. He kept walking to his room, leaving the door open. A few moments later, she entered but kept her distance.

"Are you here to make sure I don't do anything to myself?" he asked, half-joking.

"Not really," she murmured. "Magi Shabazz wanted me to give you space, but I felt you might want to talk. If you do, I'm here. If you don't, I can leave."

Akeem hesitated, but the words tumbled out. "Do you miss your family?"

She nodded. "Yeah. I think about them every day. Wonder if they're eating well, if they're safe.

I hope I never hear news that they've been taken."

"I just want to speak to mine," Akeem said, looking down at his hands. "There was this one time I got lost when I was little—ran off instead of waiting at school. My mom was terrified. When they found me, she was crying, and she hugged me so hard I couldn't breathe. Back then, I thought it was the worst thing in the world. But now… I know it was love. She felt it was too much to lose me."

"They sound like good people, but I don't think they would want you to run from this."

She was right. The way he had been brought up was to stand strong, even if it was hard.

"I just miss them," Akeem murmured. "I can't get through this alone."

"I miss mine too. But I know why I'm here, and that's to help you until you're ready to face Muovu. If I ran now, it'd ruin everything. We'd lose the fight before it even began."

Akeem studied her face. "How do you do it? This confidence in me that I can do it?"

"Because I saw it in you. You might be new here, but you have kind eyes, and I know you have a hidden strength that Alkebulan needs right now."

It comforted him a little, but only a little. Eventually, she left him alone. He lay on his bed, staring at the ceiling, exhausted. He didn't even remember falling asleep.

When Akeem opened his eyes, everything around him was on fire. He was in the middle of a street, houses blazing on all sides. The smell of smoke, charred wood, and people's screams filled the air.

Akeem staggered back as someone pushed past him. He tripped and fell, catching himself just in time to see a burned body in the street. His scream tore from his throat.

He jolted upright in bed, drenched in sweat, gasping. Footsteps thundered down the hall. Imani and Nala burst in.

"What's going on?" Imani demanded, while ordering Nala to search for intruders.

"It was just a dream," he panted. "Just a dream."

Imani gave him a worried look. "You sounded like someone was attacking you."

He ran a hand over his face. "No, it was just… I think I was too tired." He sighed. "What were you guys doing too?"

"Patrolling," Imani said and then waved at Nala, who bowed to Akeem and then walked out. She turned back to him. "Are you sure you're okay?"

"Yeah, I'm fine," Akeem said. "It's just… this place. I haven't had nightmares since I got here, but seeing those people in the city, it's like it's getting worse."

"So, what are you saying? That we should just turn back now?"

He shook his head. "No, I'm just saying it's hard. This place—it's too much sometimes."

She chuckled, but it wasn't warm. "I apologize for my words, but you've barely been here two weeks, and you're already falling apart."

"Obviously," he almost yelled out. "I was taken from my family and told I had to carry all of this."

"I know what carrying a burden feels like, but leadership isn't about being ready. It's about accepting what's asked of you. You don't get to pick the moment you're called."

Her words stung because they were true. Before he could answer, she bowed slightly. "Since you look fine, I'll leave now." She walked out, closing the door behind her.

He sat there in the darkness, staring at the door. Even if he ran, they'd find him. He couldn't outrun the prophecy or his parents' last words. He remembered what Shabash had told him about Ubuntu.

But who really was he? Akeem, the boy from Atlanta? Or the prince growing into his new role?"

He couldn't answer that. Not yet.

CHAPTER 10:

Unsettled Ground

keem woke with a dull headache pressing behind his eyes, as if the weight of everything he'd seen the day before had settled there. He lay still, haunted by the images in his nightmare.

A tray of food sat by his bed—likely from Nala. He freshened up, then picked at the tasteless meal, Imani's words echoing in his mind: "You don't get to pick the moment you're called."

A sharp knock made him jump. Nala entered with a smile. "Time for your lesson with Magi Kwame."

He sighed, pushing the plate aside. "Yeah, let's go."

They moved through hallways until Nala stopped at a carved door, opening it to a sunlit room lined with bookshelves and colorful cloths. A small balcony let in the morning breeze.

Kwame stood there, leaning on a staff. His smile was warm. "Good morning, Akeem. How are you feeling?"

Akeem gave a half-smile, sarcasm creeping in. "Morning. I'm just great." He paused, then admitted, "No. I'm not fine. But I guess I'll be fine."

Kwame nodded. "Honesty is a good place to start. Today, we'll explore the values of Alkebulan." He gestured to a woven mat on the balcony. "Sit."

Akeem obeyed, the sun on his skin making him squint. "So, are we going through books today?"

Kwame shook his head. "No, today we'll just talk. I'm going to ask you some questions—scenarios, really—and I want your honest thoughts on   each."
 Akeem furrowed his brow. "Alright."

Kwame lifted one finger. "First: You see a child stealing bread because they're hungry. The baker catches them and demands punishment. What do you do?"

Akeem thought hard. "I'd pay the baker for the bread, but that just teaches the kid that stealing is okay. If I let the baker punish them, I'm letting a hungry kid get beaten. Maybe I'd talk to both of them—ask why the baker wouldn't feed a starving child in the first place."

Kwame smiled. "Good. Empathy isn't blind charity. It's seeking the root of suffering." He held up a second finger. "Second: You see a guard taking a bribe to let a dangerous man into the city. What do you do?"

"That's betrayal—he's risking everyone's safety. I'd report him—" He hesitated. "But what if he took the bribe to feed his family? Or maybe he's being blackmailed. If I report him, I might make things worse. But if I don't, the dangerous man gets in." He shook his head. "I'd have to know why he took the bribe before I act."

Kwame's eyes glinted with approval. "Good. Justice isn't vengeance. It's understanding the whole story." He raised his third finger. "Third: You discover a friend has betrayed you, passing information to Muovu's men. What do you do?"

Akeem's gut twisted. His throat felt dry. "I—" He stopped again, wrestling with the options. "If I confront him, he might lie. If I punish him, I risk losing the trust of others who might think I'm too harsh. But if I forgive him, he could betray me again—and maybe others, too." He rubbed his forehead. "I—I don't know. Maybe I'd talk to him first. See why he did it. But even if he had a reason, can I risk keeping him around? I'd have to decide if the risk was worth it."

Kwame's expression turned solemn. "That, Akeem, is the hardest choice of all. Loyalty is a fragile thread. Sometimes, a leader cannot afford forgiveness, especially when it involves the safety of many. Wisdom is knowing that betrayal always has a cost."

Akeem's chest tightened, as if a hand was pressing down on him. "So, I failed that one?"

"It is not failure. Think of it as growth. Each answer you gave showed more than a simple reaction; it showed that you are learning to think. A leader does not always have the luxury of easy choices. Sometimes, every choice is hard."

Kwame tapped his staff on the floor once. "And now I leave you with this riddle. He leaned in: "When the storm comes and the waters rise, the tallest tree cannot hold back the flood. Yet the smallest seed is carried forward to a new land. Who is the true strength?"

Akeem stared at him, his mind whirling. "I—I don't understand."

Kwame only smiled. "You will. In time."

The riddle wound itself around his mind, over-shadowing even the dull ache in his head. He rubbed his temples. The seed? The tree? Strength? It was all a puzzle, and he didn't feel ready to solve it.

A soft sound made him turn. Shabazz stood there, silent as always. Akeem felt a flicker of resentment. He still hadn't forgiven Shabazz for hiding him from his own parents or for making him feel like a pawn.

"Shabazz," Akeem said flatly, letting his displeasure show.

Shabazz met his gaze, like he understood his anger. But he didn't say anything regarding it. "Akeem, I need you to write letters," he murmured. "Letters to the two other royal kingdoms, Wakanda and Zamunda. They've been our allies for long."

Akeem frowned. "I—I don't even know those people. Why would they listen to me?"

"You may not know them, but they know your lineage. Your parents and ancestors forged alliances with them. One day, you might need their help."

"But what if they are connected to Muovu?"

"For your first question, we've always been watching them, and they don't seem to agree with Muovu's plan. Also, there are marriage relations amongst us. They wouldn't resist these."

Akeem looked at the papers Shabazz handed him. "Today?"

"Anytime, I won't rush you."

Akeem nodded slowly, though he still felt reluctant. "Alright," he murmured. "I'll write them. But I'll do it my way."

Shabazz gave a small smile. "That would be wise. Write them as yourself. Not as a prince repeating someone else's words. Tell them who you are, what you've seen, and what you intend to do. Let them hear the voice of a leader who is both a man and a king. That's all I ask."

***

Akeem's head still buzzed from the morning's philosophy session. Kwame's riddle gnawed at his mind like an uninvited guest, refusing to leave him alone. But there wasn't time to dwell on it, as Imani was waiting in the training courtyard.

The afternoon sun cast long shadows across the sandy ground. A faint breeze stirred the hem of Akeem's tunic, but he barely felt it. Ever since that nightmare—and their heated argument— something had shifted between them. An invisible wall that neither of them wanted to cross.

With an unreadable expression, she asked, "Ready?"

Akeem nodded. "Yeah," he muttered, though he didn't feel ready at all.

"Let's begin," she murmured, stepping forward.

She guided him through the familiar stance, then into the Ankh. Her voice from their earlier lessons echoed in his head: "Breathe with purpose. Let the energy flow naturally."

He closed his eyes and inhaled slowly, focusing on his center. A warmth stirred in his core, just like she'd shown him. But something was off as his thoughts kept returning to the argument.

He felt hands on his shoulders, and suddenly his heart pounded so hard it hurt. He didn't know how to explain it, but all he knew was that he felt something in him explode outward.

A scream ripped through the air. His eyes snapped open, and he saw Imani clutching her arm, her eyes wide with pain. A thin, red line ran down her skin. His stomach dropped.

"Oh my God," he gasped, his chest seizing. Panic clawed at him as he rose. "A-Are you okay?" He reached for her, but she stepped away.

"You need to learn to control yourself," she murmured coldly, her voice trembling with anger.

"I—I don't even know what I did—" He stammered, his eyes darting to the blood, sickened by what he'd caused.

"You weren't meditating like I told you to," she snapped, her breath ragged. "Your power's too hot to handle, and you just let it burn. You need to master it before it masters you."

Then she turned and walked away, leaving him standing there.

Akeem stared at her retreating back, confused and helpless. He still didn't know what had happened, but she was right. He needed to get a grip on himself.

As the training had ended and Imani was no longer in sight, not even Nala, he began to walk back toward his quarters. Just then, he heard a sound, and he glanced behind him, half-expecting to see someone there. Nothing. Just the empty hallway.

But the feeling didn't leave him. The hairs on the back of his neck stood up. He quickened his pace, scanning everywhere. Still no one.

Where was Nala when he needed her?

He reached his room, which looked the same as he'd left it — papers still scattered across the table. He exhaled slowly, trying to calm his racing heart. Maybe he was just letting his imagination get the better of him.

Still, the unease clung to him like a second skin.

He resolved that tomorrow would be different. He'd find a way to master his emotions. And more importantly, he needed to make things right with Imani.

CHAPTER 11:

Missing Link

Akeem stumbled through the burning streets, the heat biting at his skin. Smoke choked the air, carrying the stench of scorched wood and bodies. He hadn't seen any yet, but he knew. Purple streaks of light danced between the flames. And then something new—agonizing sounds where he heard his name whispered again and again.

"Follow me," they said from everywhere and nowhere at once.

The purple lights flickered ahead, as if leading him somewhere he didn't want to go. Smoke stung his eyes, and panic clawed at him as the flames closed in, but his legs refused to stop.

Then, just ahead, the lights merged into a single, blazing ball.

He immediately woke up. For a moment, he lay in the darkness, heart pounding and body trembling. He rolled onto his side, forcing his eyes shut, hoping it would fade. But the phantom heat lingered, and he could still hear the whispers.

By the time he awoke again, the windows were open, allowing sunlight in. He blinked, half-expecting to see Nala with her smile. Instead, a girl dressed like Nala stood there—someone he barely recognized. Her eyes widened.

"My lord," she murmured, hurrying over. "Is there anything you need?"

"Um…sorry, where's Nala?"

"She's gone home for the day."

Akeem sat up fast. "She went home? I wasn't told."

"We are allowed to go home once in a while." The servant dropped her gaze. "I'll be taking her place today."

His chest tightened. Without Nala's exuberant energy, the room felt hollow. He rubbed his temples, the nightmare still echoing.

"Alright. Thanks."

He went through the motions of breakfast, but the ache in his chest didn't ease. He couldn't sit still. He needed to move. After he'd eaten, he headed toward the library, the new servant trailing behind—he couldn't remember her name.

Inside, Amani was in his usual spot, but this time he rose.

"I've been wanting to see you since that day," he murmured.

Akeem shifted uncomfortably, thinking of how he'd nearly lost his cool with Shabazz and the others.

"I'm sorry about that day—"

"No, we should be the ones apologizing," Amani cut in, surprising him. He gestured to a seat, and they both sat.

It seemed Amani was finding the words to say, and Akeem used the opportunity to study the older man's face, noticing for the first time how lined it was. All three of them—Amani, Shabazz, and Kwame—looked older than he'd imagined, though he couldn't place their ages exactly. Seventies, maybe.

Amani's face reminded him of a gentle grandfather—one who always had sweets for the kids.

When he spoke, Akeem felt at ease, like he could say what was on his mind without fear of judgment.

Shabazz was different. His stern demeanor always got under Akeem's skin, though he realized now that maybe Shabazz didn't mean to be harsh. The man rarely smiled, and even if he had, Akeem couldn't remember it.

Kwame was a bit of both—sometimes kind, sometimes cryptic. Like the riddle he'd given Akeem. He wondered if he could talk to Amani about it, but the man was already speaking.

"We thought it would be simple," Amani began. "Take you to a safe place and prepare you to face your destiny. But we forgot you're human too." His voice softened. "We've helped royal families and warriors achieve their goals, even those who doubted us. But you... you fight us at every turn." He sighed. "Still, we should've understood you better. I'm sorry for everything that's happened."

Akeem went quiet, not because he lacked words, but because it was one of those rare cases where an adult apologized to him. Also in that moment, he realized something:

He'd been acting like a child.

Truthfully, his anger was justified. He'd been taken from his family, and he missed them. But the general consensus was that he was also the heir of Alkebulan.

"I know you didn't mean to hurt me," he murmured softly. "I'll try to understand it all better."

Amani nodded, and for a moment they shared an understanding. Then he cleared his throat, slipping into teacher mode.

"Now, about what you read about your parents, any questions?"

Akeem hesitated. The memories of his parents felt so close, yet so far. He'd seen them in a new light and didn't know where to begin.

"Yeah," he murmured. "I guess I was surprised about how they met. I thought my dad was of the royal family, but he wasn't, and he just threw himself in front of a blade for my mother. That's... wow."

Amani leaned forward. "Your father's path wasn't easy. Serving in the Sentinel Guard is a lifetime commitment. It means protecting others at any cost. That he was willing to die for your mother speaks to his honor. And your mother's royal line has always been more than blood. She earned her crown. That's why the people loved her."

"I read something about her being connected to the ancestral spirits. What's that about?"

Amani's eyes lit up. "Ah, that's one of the most sacred parts of Alkebulan's royal tradition. Every heir must undergo spiritual tests to prove their worthiness. It's not just about strength or wisdom; it's about being guided by the ancestors. That's part of the training you're doing now with Imani."

"Wait," Akeem said. "You mean voices of the dead?"

"It's a way of saying that a true ruler carries the wisdom and strength of all those who led before them. It's a bond, forged through rituals, meditation, even visions."

The last part made Akeem want to ask about his nightmares, but he decided to be patient and ask the most pressing question. "Why did Muovu betray the kingdom? What's he after?"

Amani's expression darkened. "Muovu wants to use the Alkeic stones to build his war machine and tighten his grip on power. He's even rumored to be making deals with foreign nations, though we don't have proof yet. His dream is to turn Alkebulan into a superpower, but it's driven by greed. He hated your parents' vision of what the royal family should be, and he stole it from them."

"Wow. I wish I knew all of these before."

"It would have been too much for you," Amani responded. "Some stories are best hidden until the right time. Also, prophecies can be dangerous. They shape how people see you, sometimes more than your own actions."

Akeem nodded slowly. "Yeah, I get that." He paused, then added, "Back in Atlanta, we didn't have anything like this. Everything was about climbing the ladder. If you wanted to stand out, you had to outshine everyone else. No prophecies were telling you who you were gonna be."

"That's fascinating. Here, we believe the ancestors shape us. But you—" He smiled softly. "You grew up in a place where you shape yourself."

"Yeah," Akeem murmured. "But sometimes… I don't know who I'm supposed to be."

"That's a question every leader must answer. Maybe it's not about who you're supposed to be but who you choose to become."

Akeem took a deep breath and then, returning to his other question, he asked, "Actually, I've been having some nightmares lately that I don't understand. I don't know if they are related to the visions you mentioned."

"You should talk to Shabazz about that. He's the best one to help."

Later, after the lesson, Akeem found his guard waiting outside. "Hey," he murmured. "Do you know where Shabazz's office is?"

"Yes, my lord. I can take you there."

"Thank you."

They walked down the corridor, turned left, and reached a door. Akeem knocked and pushed it open.

Shabazz looked up from a stack of papers. "Prince Akeem," he murmured, nodding.

Akeem had been called so many names lately that a new one didn't make him flinch anymore.

"How can I help you?" Shabazz continued.

"I heard Nala went home," Akeem said, stepping inside.

The office was smaller than he expected, walls lined with heavy wooden shelves packed with scrolls, jars of herbs, and objects that glowed faintly. A large, worn desk dominated the center, cluttered with open books, a few tablets, and a half-burned candle. A faint scent of sandalwood and old paper filled the air.

"Yes, it was her time to go home. She'll be back tomorrow," Shabazz said, gesturing to a chair. "Want to sit?"

Akeem shook his head. "I just came because Amani suggested it." He exhaled shakily. "I've been having nightmares. And… something happened with my power. Imani got hurt. I didn't mean to. I just…" He ran a hand through his hair. "I don't know how to handle all this."

"Tell me everything."

And he did. Shabazz listened quietly. When Akeem finished, the old Magi's eyes softened.

"Imani told me about the incident," he murmured. "Nightmares can mean many things—stress, power you haven't mastered, fears you haven't faced. Right now, yours are linked to your bottled melanic energy."

"I don't understand that."

"Your melanic energy is tied to your bloodline. It's your strength, but it's also raw. When you suppress it or refuse to face your feelings, that energy turns inward. It builds until it spills out like in your nightmares, or with Imani."

Akeem's stomach twisted. "So… the nightmares are my fault?"

Shabazz shook his head. "Not your fault. But they're a reflection of what's inside you. They show what you haven't faced yet. Think of them as a guide, not a curse. Face them, and you'll grow."

"But how?"

"Control," Shabazz said. "Let your power flow, but don't let it rule you. Meditate on the dreams, ask yourself what they mean, and face what you fear most. Only then will your melanic energy obey you."

Akeem nodded. "I'll try. I need to see Imani too."

"Good, but first, there's something I want to show you."

Shabazz rose and led Akeem out of the office, down the corridor, where there was a flight of stairs. They climbed it, the air cooling as they rose. At the top, Shabazz pushed open the door. Akeem expected shelves of books or scrolls, but his breath caught.

The room was massive with gleaming, polished floors. Glass panels lined the walls, revealing rows of workstations buzzing with activity. People in uniforms moved between circuit boards and glowing screens filled with shifting code.

Akeem's eyes darted to familiar shapes—processors, cooling systems, even holographic projectors—intermixed with devices he couldn't name.

"This… this is incredible," he whispered.

Shabazz smiled. "This is the tech center. Smaller than what we had in Alkebulan, but it's a start. We're rebuilding and trying to preserve what we can."

Akeem's gaze swept the room, and a thrill ran through him. His degree in computer programming suddenly felt useful. Shabazz didn't introduce him—Akeem was grateful for that—and none of the engineers seemed to notice who he was.

They moved deeper into the room. Akeem spotted a table where a group of engineers hovered over a boxy machine with blinking lights and exposed wiring. Sparks flickered at its side, and frustration lined their faces.

Akeem's eyes widened. "That's a multipurpose data unit. We used them for network bridging back in Atlanta."

One of the engineers, with a familiar face, turned. "You know this tech?"

Akeem hesitated, his hands itching to dive in. "Yeah," he murmured. "I think I can help." He leaned over, adjusted a few wires, and tapped the control pad. The machine hummed and then sparked with a pop.

He flinched, cheeks burning. "Sorry, I thought I had it."

Before the embarrassment could sink deeper, Shabazz spoke. "Our prince is still learning," he murmured, addressing the room. "Please, forgive him."

The engineers' mouths dropped, and they all bowed deeply. Akeem sputtered. "Uh—thank you," he managed.

They nodded and returned to their work.

Akeem turned to Shabazz. "Thank you. I still want to help, though. I think I can do something."

Shabazz rested a hand on his shoulder. "The door is always open. And believe me, we need every bright mind we can get."

***

After leaving the tech center, Akeem's head buzzed with images of machines and engineers. But a new worry tugged at him — Imani.

He searched the halls and the training yard, but she was nowhere. Maybe she was avoiding him; after what happened earlier, he wouldn't blame her. Still, she was supposed to train him. She wouldn't just disappear… would she?

He sighed and made his way to the training yard. The sun hung low, painting the sand in a burnt orange glow. In a quiet corner, he tried again to channel his energy into the Ankh transfer. He focused on his breath, reaching for that pulse of power, but it kept slipping through his fingers.

Yet even in his frustration, he felt a strange peace, like a weight had lifted. He wasn't getting it right, but at least he felt grounded.

Finally, he trudged back to his room. When he opened the door, he was startled — and relieved — to see Nala waiting.

Her eyes were apologetic. "My lord, I'm sorry I left without telling you. It was sudden, and there was no time."

He smiled faintly. "I'm just glad you're here now."

He moved toward his desk, but Nala stepped forward, stopping him.

"There's something I need to give you," she murmured.

"What is it?"

She held out a small device, which oddly looked like a phone and a calculator at the same time.

"With this," she whispered, "you can finally call your parents."

Akeem's chest tightened. He immediately forgot how to breathe as he stared at the device, everything else momentarily forgotten.

CHAPTER 12:

Missing Link

Akeem stared at the device in his hands, unable to speak for a long moment. Finally, he found his voice.

"When did you get this?" he asked, his eyes searching hers.

She smiled in a way that suggested he might not get a straight answer.

"I got it for you," she murmured instead. "When I went home to my family, I realized I didn't understand what it was like for you, being here without yours. It's one thing to have your family near and another to be cut off completely. I realized how lonely you must feel. So, I brought this back for you."

Akeem shook his head. "No, that's not what I meant. I mean—thank you. Really. I'm glad." He let out a shaky laugh. "But… how did you get it? Shabazz refused me so many times, and I doubt he would've given it to you."

She looked down for a long moment, then shook her head. "I'm sorry, my lord. This is one thing I can't give you a clear answer on. But if I did wrong—" She looked up, her eyes shining. "—I understand if you don't want it. I just wanted to help. You've been locked up in here, not even allowed to call your parents. With this, you can hear their voices and know they're okay. But if you'd rather not…"

She moved to slip the device back into her pocket, but Akeem grabbed her wrist, stopping her.

"Wait," he murmured.

At the back of his mind, he knew he shouldn't. But the thought of hearing his parents' voices overpowered his hesitation. She'd gone through so much to get it. He couldn't just let that go.

"But where did you get this from, though?" He took it from her hands.

She flashed a bright smile. "It doesn't matter. You can use it tonight, then I'll take it back and return it. You won't have to worry about a thing."

He turned the device over in his hands, studying the odd buttons and black screen. "How do I even use it? I've never seen anything like this before."

"It's like a phone," she explained, her fingers grazing over the smooth surface. "Just tap in the number and call. It's simple. We use it for external communication sometimes, and it's untraceable."

"Like… I can call, and no one can find out where I am?"

"Exactly."

She gave him a small bow and left the room. He sat on his bed, holding it to his chest as the weight of what he held settled into his bones. Should he use it or not? Just one button, and he could hear their voices again. Or he could hide it away, pretend it didn't exist, and never risk the consequences.

Shabazz's warning echoed in his head — secrecy above all else. And yet, they'd never asked him what he wanted, only what he could do for them. And then, he thought of Nala's assurances.

Still, he decided not to rush it. He slipped it under his pillow — somewhere no one would think to look.

He tried to read to distract himself, but the symbols blurred together as his mind drifted back to the device. Finally, he set the book aside and grabbed a quick meal. Nala was close by, giving nothing away as if trained to keep secrets. He also didn't dare talk to her about it, knowing that even the walls here had ears.

That night, he didn't use the device. Instead, he lay on his back, staring at the ceiling until sleep took him.

When he woke, he was no longer in his room. He was back in his old bedroom in Atlanta, staring up at the familiar brown ceiling. It felt so real he had to pinch his arm, feeling the sharp twinge. He pushed back the covers and stepped out into the hallway, his breath catching at the sight of his parents in the living room. He tried to call out to them, but his voice wouldn't come. They didn't even see him.

The scene shifted. Now he stood at the kitchen doorway, watching them cook together. He longed to join them, but his legs were rooted to the ground. He felt like a ghost watching a world he no longer belonged to. He reached out, groaning as he stumbled forward—only to have the floor open beneath him. He fell into an endless darkness.

He woke with a jolt, heart pounding. This time, he knew what he had to do.

His hand shot under his pillow, trembling as it closed around the device. Quietly, he slipped into the small restroom, locked the door, and stood in front of the mirror. He tapped in his mother's number and pressed the green button. The line rang.

No answer.

He tried again. Just as he was sure someone would burst in and accuse him of betrayal, a voice came through.

"Hello?"

He froze, pressing a shaking hand to his mouth, uncertain if it was the device or a voice just beyond the door.

"Hello?" the voice asked again.

"It's me, Ma," he whispered, tears welling in his eyes.

Silence fell, then a trembling voice answered. "Akeem? Is it really you?"

His throat tightened as tears spilled down his cheeks. "Yeah, Ma. It's me."

"Oh, Akeem, baby, how — how did you call? They told us we couldn't talk to you."

"I — I got a device," he stammered. "I just wanted to hear your voice. I wanted to know you're okay."

"Oh, baby, we're fine. We've been trying to reach you, too, but Shabazz said it wasn't allowed and told us not to call again. He said it'd be a distraction."

A stone lodged itself in his chest. That's not what Shabazz told him.

"What?" he asked, confused.

"Is there a problem?"

He hesitated, knowing she couldn't see his face. "Don't worry about that. I just needed to hear your voice."

"Oh, Akeem," she sighed. "Your father and I talk about you every day. Sometimes it's hard, but we know you have a purpose there."

He clenched his teeth, a bitter ache creeping into his chest. They all sounded so willing to trust people he didn't even know.

Then his father's voice came on. "Akeem? Is that you?"

"Yeah, Dad," he croaked. "It's me."

"I'm so glad to hear from you, son. As long as you're safe, that's all that matters."

"Y-yeah."

His mother spoke again, her tone softer now. "Akeem, we have to go, but please remember: we love you. We wish you success always."

His throat tightened, and the words caught in his chest. "I love you, too," he whispered.

The call ended abruptly, leaving a hollow silence. Akeem sank to his knees, the air around him seeming to close. His breaths came shallow. For a long moment, he stayed there, shaking, until something unexpected happened.

Purple streaks weaving through white sparks appeared, swirling around his hands like living ribbons. He stared, mesmerized, as if a part of him was awakening. Then, as suddenly as it had come, the light vanished, leaving him stunned.

Blinking away the tears, he went back to the room and tucked the device back under his pillow. Sleep wouldn't come. Instead, he sat at his desk and turned his focus to the problem at the tech center. Hours passed before he finally found the solution. When he collapsed into bed, exhaustion pulled him under.

The next morning, his head felt clearer. He spotted Nala and gave her a bright smile, which she returned. It felt like a scene out of a play: the prince and his loyal guard.

As he ate breakfast, he thought of the device still under his pillow. He'd give it to her that morning and then head to the tech center.

Walking through the hallway just outside his room, he paused. "Thank you so much for helping me. I don't know how you did it, but… thank you," he murmured.

Nala smiled softly. "You're welcome, my lord."

He stepped into the room, reached under his pillow to hand her the device, and froze. It wasn't there. His heart as he turned to Nala.

For the first time, he saw fear flicker across her face.

CHAPTER 13:

A Price Paid

"It was right here," Akeem said. "I remember putting it here."

Nala stepped closer, scanning the floor. "Don't worry. I'll find it."

"No—"

"If you skip your lessons, they'll know something's wrong. Just go. I'll handle this."

"Are you sure?" he asked, concerned.

She smiled, though it seemed shaky. "I've been through worse. Trust me. Just go."

Reluctantly, he turned away. His heart pounded with nerves and doubt. Could she handle it on her own? Still, she was right—if he stayed, he'd only get into more trouble.

He headed down the hall and then up the stairs. Opening the door, an engineer looked up and bowed to him. "Good morning, my lord. Do you need some help?"

"Last time I was here, there was a problem. Has it been fixed?"

"We're working on it," the engineer assured him.

"Okay, but I think I've got an idea, not a full fix, though, but I want to try something."

He was led to the same spot as before, where the engineer who had struck him as familiar glanced up, surprised.

"My lord," he murmured, "what are you doing here?"

"I'm here because of the issue from last time," Akeem explained, fumbling a bit. "I think I have a… solution to try."

They all exchanged curious glances. He felt like he was back in class, trying to explain himself.

"Let me try," Akeem repeated. "If it doesn't work, I'll step aside."

The engineers nodded. He focused on the device, following the plan in his mind. Slowly, it began to warm. The engineers stepped back and cheered.

The engineer came closer, bowing his head. "I'm Akili Mensah, one of the lead engineers here. Thank you so much for your help."

"No, thank you," Akeem replied, studying Akili's face. Something about him reminded Akeem of Imani.

He hesitated, then asked, "Are you… related to Imani?"

Akili smiled, a spark in his eyes. "Yes, I'm her younger brother."

Akeem nodded slowly, finally placing the connection. Just then, Akili looked behind him, and Akeem turned to see Imani at the door, watching them with a surprised expression. He approached her, and she returned a faint smile, curiosity woven through it.

"Good day, my lord. May I ask what brings you here?" she murmured.

Akeem wasn't sure if she was annoyed that he knew or just cautious after their last meeting. Still, he pressed on.

"Shabazz brought me here yesterday. Said I might want to see this place," he murmured, glancing toward her brother, who was deep in conversation with the engineers. "He's smart."

Imani smiled faintly, and that was it.

He continued. "Also, I'd like to apologize for not listening to you. You were right." He glanced at her arm, but she was wearing a long-sleeved white shirt, which hid them.

She nodded slightly. "It's no problem."

"But why didn't you tell me you had a brother?"

"I don't like to talk about my family, and also, we are supposed to focus on your training."

"Well, I looked for you yesterday, but you were nowhere."

"I wasn't exactly available yesterday, as there were some things I needed to handle. But I'm available now."

And then she turned away, and he followed her to the training yard.

"I'd like to see you try the Ankh method again and this time, clear your mind," she murmured.

Akeem sat down, drawing in the energy he'd practiced so many times. This time, he didn't overthink it. Instead, he focused on that beacon he had seen in his dreams, drawn to its immense light.

A quiet clap broke the silence. Opening his eyes, he saw purple and white light dancing around his body before fading away.

Imani gave him a small smile, looking pleased. "Looks like you've been practicing. You're starting to control it, which is not perfect yet, but it's progress. You can keep practicing any time you get. Now, on to the next step."

From a bag, she laid out a smooth Alkeic stone, a scroll marked with ancient symbols, and a slender staff etched with similar designs.

Akeem's eyes widened. "I think I've seen these symbols before in one of the books," he murmured, crouching to study the scroll. "But I couldn't make sense of them back then."

Imani folded her arms. "These are the Solomonic Scrolls, which are keys to harnessing Karbo Kosmic. The Alkeic stone you see acts as a conduit, and that staff is an amplifier. It focuses your energy."

Akeem looked up. "It allows me to use my powers?"

"Not just using them." She shook her head. "Right now, your abilities are small compared to what they could be. But by practicing and learning to blend Kemetic knowledge, the Solomonic Scrolls, and the Alkeic stones, you'll grow stronger. The Ankh transfer you learned was just the first step."

Akeem reached for the stone and held it in his palm. It felt warm and alive. He closed his eyes, trying to sense the energy he'd been practicing. A low hum tickled his fingers—faint, but there.

"That's good," Imani's voice came softly. "You're learning to sense the flow. Don't expect to master it in a day, but you're already ahead because of your Ankh transfer."

Akeem opened his eyes and grinned. "So, when are we gonna spar though?"

Imani raised an eyebrow, amused. "You seem… eager."

"Yeah," he admitted. "I think I finally understand why I'm here. I want to change. I want to get stronger."

She opened her mouth to reply, but a guard hurried up the path, eyes darting between them. "Apologies, my lord," he murmured, out of breath. "Magi Shabazz is asking for you."

Imani turned back to Akeem. "We'll continue this later."

"Alright," he murmured, nodding.

He dropped the stone and followed the guard down the corridor to Shabazz's office. The door swung open, revealing Shabazz standing by his desk. Akeem's gaze fell on the device resting there—his device—and his heart pounded.

He tried to calm himself and stepped forward. "You called for me?"

Shabazz's expression was unreadable. "I think you know why you're here."

Akeem weighed his options: lie or own up to it. Looking at the device and knowing what he'd done, he decided to be honest. "Yes," he murmured quietly. "I made the call. I needed to hear from them to know they were okay."

Shabazz's eyes darkened. "Even after I warned you?"

"Yes," Akeem said, lifting his chin. "I know it was wrong, but you wouldn't let me speak to them. They told me they'd tried to call, but you said I was too busy. Why would you do that to me?"

"To protect you!" Shabazz's voice rose. "The goal was to shield you, Prince Akeem, not to throw you to the wolves. I told you your parents would be fine and that they knew you were safe. You should have trusted me. I could've arranged a proper call, but you defied me."

Akeem clenched his fists. "I get it. I messed up. But nothing happened; no one got hurt."

Shabazz leaned in, his face hard. "Nothing happened because we made sure nothing did. Once you made that call, there was a signal. If Muovu's men had intercepted that call, we'd all be in danger. His dark army would've overrun this place. You can't keep drawing attention to yourself."

"His dark army?"

"Yes, we've received word that he's building a dark army fueled by corrupted powers. His strength doesn't come from the same light that we use. It's twisted, dark, and he'll stop at nothing to get to you."

Akeem's stomach dropped. "So, he knows I'm here?"

"Not yet, but he's smart and now he knows what you are. That's why you must stop drawing attention. Please, Prince Akeem, don't make this harder than it already is."

A heavy silence settled between them. Akeem's mind raced, trying to process what he'd just heard. His eyes flicked to Shabazz, who wasn't looking at him but instead stared at something just above his head.

He finally sighed. "I'm sorry," he murmured. "I just… I needed a chance to connect." And then he paused, remembering something. "Wait. How did you get the device? Were you spying on me?"

"We picked up a signal from the tech center. It came from your quarters, and I knew immediately. I found it there, under your pillow. You were asleep and didn't even notice when it fell to the floor."

Akeem winced, ashamed. "I'm sorry," he murmured again, this time more quietly. "I—I took it from your office when I was leaving." He didn't even care if the lie sounded weak; he just needed to say it.

Shabazz's eyes met his. "You don't have to say it. Nala already told me she took it. She's been reassigned."

Akeem's heart sank. "What—wait? She did nothing wrong."

"I know," Shabazz said, his tone surprisingly gentle. He circled around the desk and sank into the chair, rubbing his forehead. "Akeem, one thing you need to understand: mistakes never go unpunished. You can be sorry for the rest of your life, but it won't erase what happened. I didn't punish Nala; I simply reassigned her. You'll have another guard soon. That's how these things work."

Akeem swallowed hard. "So… that's it?"

"That's it," Shabazz replied. "Now go. And next time, trust me enough to wait."

Akeem looked at him, a sour taste rising in his mouth, but he couldn't argue. Half of him wanted to fight, but the other half knew Shabazz was right. He turned and left the office, the hallways feeling colder than before.

But he couldn't go back to his room. Not now. Instead, his feet carried him down the corridors until he found himself back at the training yard.

There, Imani stood under the sun, doing some sparring moves—her movements swift and sharp. Akeem paused for a moment, watching her, admiring the way she seemed so sure of herself, so unbreakable.

He wanted that.

Drawing in a breath, he stepped into the yard. "I want to spar," he called.

She turned, surprise flashing in her eyes. "Oh? You've already finished your lessons for the day."

"I know," he murmured. "But I want to spar. I need to spar."

Imani paused, her gaze studying his face as though searching for something deeper. Finally, she gave a small nod. "Alright, then," she murmured. "Let's see what you've got."

She walked over to a weapons rack and pulled down a slender staff carved from dark wood. She flipped it in her hand, then held it out to him. "Here. Let's start with this."

Akeem took the staff, feeling its weight in his palms. He tried to steady his breathing as he positioned himself across from Imani, who watched him with an unreadable expression.

"Remember what I taught you," she murmured, settling into a defensive stance. "Flow with the movement. Don't force it."

He nodded and tried to mimic her posture, but as soon as she advanced, his grip faltered. The staff felt too stiff. She came at him with a smooth, fluid motion, and he tried to parry, but his swing was clumsy. She knocked his staff aside effortlessly, sending him stumbling.

"Again," she murmured.

He set his feet and tried again, but each time she moved, she was a step ahead. His strikes were too wild, and his defenses were too slow. Sweat beaded on his forehead.

"Focus on your balance," Imani urged.

But the more he tried, the worse it got. Finally, with one last clumsy swing, he lost his grip on the staff entirely. It clattered to the ground.

He stood there, chest heaving, rage and shame mixing in his gut.

Imani lowered her staff. "That's enough for today," she murmured softly. "You're pushing too hard."

Akeem glared at the staff on the ground, then turned on his heel and stormed out of the yard, unable to bear the look in her eyes.

That night, he sat alone in the dining hall. The warm scent of spiced meat and rice filled the air, but he barely tasted his food. His new royal aide—the young woman from before—had brought in the food, her presence reminding him that Nala had been reassigned because of him.

His appetite vanished. Pushing the plate away, he returned to his room. That night, as he lay in bed, he couldn't shake the feeling that he'd failed more than himself.

When sleep finally came, it dragged him into a dream.

This time, though, it felt even different. He found himself standing near the beacon of purple and white light that seemed to pulse with an other-worldly energy. Shadows stretched across the ground, and there were voices—distant at first, but growing louder.

He turned to his left and saw a figure standing there, its face obscured. He turned to his right and saw another figure, but their presence felt comforting. He couldn't explain it.

Then a voice called his name, not from the shadows, but from those two figures themselves.

"Akeem…"

He woke up, sweat soaking his back.

Shabazz's advice about writing it down. Akeem rolled out of bed, grabbed his notebook from the table, and began to write — his hand trembling, but his mind focused.

If he could make sense of these dreams, maybe he could fix what he'd broken. Maybe he could help Nala get her job back, and maybe Shabazz wouldn't have to punish anyone else.

CHAPTER 14:

Stone and Sword

For the first time, Akeem reached the training yard before Imani. She didn't know he was there yet, but he'd woken up that morning with a resolve: today, he'd prove he was serious.

Standing in the middle of the yard, staff in hand, he tried to recall the moves she had shown him. However, his swings were off-balance, and his stance was stiff. Just as he made another move, he felt the presence of someone and abruptly turned to see Imani leaning against a post, eyes wide. She coughed immediately, as if trying to hide that she was watching, and began moving towards him.

"You're doing it all wrong."

He lowered the staff, cheeks warm. "I know," he admitted. "I was just… trying to practice."

Imani raised an eyebrow. "You're here early. I usually have to come find you."

"Yeah, I figured I'd change that," he murmured, scratching his head. "I hope I'm not wasting your time."

She shook her head, a small smile appearing on her face. "No. Actually, I was about to come get you. But first, we need to go over the art of Kemistry again."

From her small bag, which she dropped onto the ground, she pulled out the Alkeic stones, smooth and glowing faintly in the early light. "You have to keep practicing with these. They connect our Kemetic knowledge with our own energy."

Akeem looked at the stones in her hand. "So… can these be used as a source of power?"

"Yes, that's one of their main purposes."

There was an idea forming in his mind, but he couldn't give it words. Instead, he took a stone from her, feeling its warmth pulse in his hand. He closed his eyes, trying to find the same focus he had yesterday. Once. Twice. By the third try, this time with eyes open, the glow flickered in his palm.

"Good," Imani said. "You're learning fast."

A grin spread across his face. "Thanks, Imani."

She gave a quick nod, her half-smile brightening her features. "You can keep practicing with the stones later. Now, we spar, this time focusing on Engolo."

She stepped back, staff in hand, moving with a grace that made Akeem's breath catch. "Engolo is more than fighting," she murmured. "It's a dance of the body and the spirit. Watch me."

She moved in a slow, twisting rhythm, her hips flowing like water as she balanced the staff behind her shoulders. Akeem tried to mirror her, but his movements were clumsy, his staff slipping out of place.

"Again, loosen your hips," she murmured, moving closer. She reached for him, her fingers brushing against his arm as she guided his stance. His pulse quickened at her touch.

"Like this." Her voice came in softly.

For a moment, their faces were inches apart. He looked into her brown eyes, feeling something unspoken pass between them. Just then, she turned away quickly and coughed lightly.

"Let's — let's do it again," she murmured in a firm voice.

Akeem adjusted his grip on the staff, drawing a breath to calm himself. Then he remembered something. "The first time I saw you, I saw these lights around you. Is that what you're trying to teach me?"

Imani paused. "You saw that?"

"Yeah," he murmured. "I've never seen anything like it."

"Yes, because that was Engolo, and in time, you should be able to do it." A small smile touched her lips. "You have the gift, but remember, you have to be intentional about it."

He nodded. "I want to learn all of it."

"Then we'll stay here until you get the basics down."

They trained for over an hour — Akeem's longest session yet. Sweat dripped down his face as he struggled through each step, his muscles burning. Sometimes, Imani corrected his stance, her hands warm against his arms, sending ripples of half excitement, half confusion through him.

Finally, they both dropped to the ground, chests heaving.

Imani smiled, strands of her hair sticking to her forehead. "That's all for today."

He nodded, wiping his brow. "Thanks, Imani."

She gave him a soft look. "Go get some rest. We'll continue later." She stood, grabbed her bag, and walked away.

Akeem lingered a moment, then pushed himself up and headed to his room. He washed up quickly, then sat at his desk, staring at the papers. He also needed to talk to Shabazz — might as well kill two birds with one stone.

Shabazz had told him to just write from the heart. But he suspected Shabazz would rewrite it anyway, making it sound all formal. Still, he picked up his pen, took a deep breath, and started.

Since the letter was going to two kingdoms, he decided to write the same one for both. He started with Wakanda.

"Royal Palace of Wakanda, Greetings," he wrote. "I greet you in peace and strength. I am Akeem Maleek of Alkebulan, and though my journey as heir is new, I already feel the weight of what befalls me. I know you stood by us even when Muovu took the throne. Thank you for standing with us then.

"Now, as I prepare to reclaim Alkebulan, I need your help more than ever. When the time comes, I hope you'll stand with us again."

He signed it—"Akeem Maleek, Heir to Alkebulan"—and set it aside to copy the same message for the other kingdom.

Once he'd finished both, he carried the letters to Shabazz's office. The old man looked up from his papers, relief washing over his face.

"Ah, you've brought them," Shabazz said, taking the letters from his hand. "Good work, Prince Akeem."

Akeem hesitated, then blurted, "Shabazz, I have a question."

He looked up. "What is it?"

Akeem took a deep breath. "I've been thinking. Maybe I should focus more on tech. I could help a lot of people. I'm not sure I'm good enough at combat to face Muovu."

Shabazz set the papers aside. "You feel that way because it's easier to hide behind machines than face the world outside."

Akeem's jaw tightened. "That's not fair. I just—"

"It is fair," Shabazz interrupted. "Your father was the same. He thought his mind was his greatest weapon, and it was. But even he had to learn the sword and the staff. Why? Because to be a leader—to protect others—you have to be strong in all things, not just the easy ones."

Akeem clenched his fists. "But with the tech, I could build things that matter."

"And fighting Muovu isn't?" Shabazz's voice turned somber. "War isn't won by machines alone. One day, you'll stand between your people and the darkness. If all you have is a machine, you'll fail them."

Akeem swallowed hard. He hadn't thought of that.

Shabazz leaned forward. "Engolo is more than a dance, Prince Akeem. It's a promise that you'll fight when your people need you most. It's about respect, survival, and leadership."

There was silence for a moment.

"You'll find your place in tech, but don't forget who you're meant to be."

"Understood," Akeem said quietly and then headed back to his room.

But on impulse, he turned and went to the library, gathering books on Wakanda and Zamunda. He realized it had been foolish to send letters to kingdoms he barely knew. Back in his room, he began flipping through stories of warriors and ancient alliances.

Time passed until a knock at the door startled him. He looked up to see his guard.

"Prince Akeem," she murmured, "the chief guard is asking for you."

His heart gave a small leap as he left his desk, and at the door was Imani, this time dressed in a top and jeans, her staff across her back.

"I don't know if you would like to come with me somewhere?" she asked.

"Of course," Akeem said, curiosity sparking, as they began walking down the hallway. "Where to?"

She shook her head. "It's a surprise."

They left the sanctuary doors and entered the forest. The air was cool, leaves whispering overhead. They walked in silence until Akeem finally asked, "You're still not going to tell me?"

Eyes ahead, she murmured, "Patience, Prince Akeem. We're close."

He hesitated. "Can't you just call me Akeem? I think we are now beyond that—"

She turned, her smile gone. "It's against the rule." She faced forward again, and they continued.

At last, the trees thinned and a clearing opened. In the center rose a massive stone structure, vines dancing around it.

Akeem stopped, awe in his voice. "What is this place?"

Imani stepped closer. "The Zion Temple," she murmured. "One of the oldest in Alkebulan. Warriors and scholars come here to train, reflect, and connect with the ancestors. I heard you'd be brought here later, but I was already coming and thought you might want to see it too."

Akeem felt a warmth inside. She'd thought about him. He stared at the carved figures on the walls — warriors, kings, queens — while the smell drifted through the air.

"But are we even supposed to be here?" he asked. "Wouldn't someone find us?"

She shook her head. "Muovu would never come here. What he wants isn't here, and there aren't many people around. We're safe."

She guided him inside, and Akeem was struck by how much larger the structure felt up close. The space opened around him, with towering walls. They found a place near a quiet corner, not far from the altar where candles — some flickering, others off — cast a wavering glow. Akeem settled onto the floor, with questions bubbling up in his mind.

"Imani," he began, "if you don't mind me asking, I heard you've been training since you were a child. What was it like… before all this?"

She stared at the candles. "It wasn't easy." Her answer came unexpectedly, as Akeem hadn't thought she would answer, and he looked at her intently, not wanting to miss anything. "My parents died young. I trained at the temple with the royal guard. Akili was more into tech, and he's been there since we moved."

"Nala said your mother served mine. Did she…?" He faltered, not sure how to ask.

Imani frowned. "Nala talks a lot."

"She murmured you didn't want her as my aide—something about her talking my ears off."

She chuckled, and he did too.

Then she sighed. "Yes, my mother served yours. The night of the attack, my mother didn't die. She was hurt, presumed dead, but found her way home. My father had been sick, so he was there to care for her, especially since she was pregnant with me."

Akeem's eyes widened. "And she fought?"

"She wasn't due yet—just a few months along. The plan had been to strike Muovu first, but the coup came too soon." She paused. "My mother had me, but she was never the same. My father raised me. Three years later, she recovered enough to have my brother, but she died soon after. He never really knew her."

His chest tightened.

"I wanted to follow her path," she continued. "My father was scared but taught me the basics, and I learned quickly. We didn't know Muovu was hunting down every family tied to the old guard. Our house was burned, and only my brother and I survived. The Magi found us, took us in. They taught me to fight and be strong."

Akeem leaned forward. "I'm so sorry."

"Thank you," she murmured quietly. "But I didn't tell you for pity. It's my life, and it's made me who I am. I only look back to draw strength from it."

He studied her face, the candlelight dancing in her eyes. He wished he were like her—steady, unflinching, able to set her pain aside like a blade on a rack. He, on the other hand, felt like his own fire threatened to consume him from the inside, leaving behind ashes.

A silence fell between them. Akeem shifted uncomfortably, searching for a lighter subject.

"So..." he ventured, voice tentative, "did you... ever have someone? Someone you cared about?"

A muscle in her jaw twitched. "Those are questions you shouldn't ask me, my lord."

My lord. The way she murmured it felt like a wall slamming shut.

"Forgive my intrusion," he murmured quickly. "I was just curious."

She stood abruptly, the fragile moment slipping through his fingers like sand. He scrambled to his feet, too.

"It's alright," she murmured, her smile a mask now. "I think it's better we leave."

Akeem felt a twinge of regret deep in his chest. "Alright."

They left the temple and made their way back. At the building's entrance, she disappeared into the shadows, off to wherever she went when she wasn't training him. He realized with a pang that he didn't even know.

Back in his room, he tried to focus on his reading, but the words blurred on the page. He thought about the conversation they'd had about the Alkeic stones — how they might hold the key to unlocking Alkebulan's future. He needed to understand.

He made his way to the library, hoping to find Amani, but found it empty. So, he hunted through the shelves until he found a thick volume on the stones' history and technological uses.

In his room, he devoured the pages and began jotting. But fatigue crept in, heavier than he could fight. His head drooped, and sleep claimed him.

And then he was back in that dream again — only this time, he was standing before the beacon of light, and a voice called his name clearly.

"Akeem."

He turned to his left, and there stood King Jabari, looking very much alive.

CHAPTER 15:

Footsteps in the Dark

For a moment, Akeem said nothing, staring at the apparition dressed in a king's clothing. He even wore a crown. It felt too real to be a trick of his mind. Then the figure opened its mouth and said his name again. Akeem stumbled back, mouth open.

He had never spoken to anyone in his dreams before, especially not someone who was long dead. He shook his head, his voice cracking. "Is this real?"

King Jabari's expression softened. "Not exactly. It's somewhere between real and not real, a space between the waking world and the dream. In this space, I can talk to you."

Akeem glanced around, noticing the smell of charred bodies and burnt buildings was gone. Even the sound of distant voices had vanished. They were alone, standing before a blazing beacon of light that no longer felt hot.

"How is this even possible?"

He raised a hand. "Careful with that question. If you think too hard about it, you might get stuck in something you can't pull yourself out of. Just know this is a safe place, and we can talk."

"But you're dead."

He realized, then, that this was the first time he'd really seen his father—holograms never did justice to the man before him now. It was like staring into a mirror: the same nose, the same eyes, the same build. It was uncanny.

King Jabari shook his head. "You're asking the wrong questions. Ask me anything else you've ever wanted to know."

Akeem fell silent, his mind churning. Jabari just watched him, with a patient expression.

Finally, the older man spoke, as if knowing it was overwhelming for him. "I'm sure you would have wondered about my life when I became king, but I would like to mention that I never planned to be. I just wanted to be a good man—take care of my family and maybe find a sweet woman to share my life with. Then I met your mother, and everything changed. Sometimes your destiny doesn't care what you want."

He paused, and his gaze met Akeem's. "I never imagined we'd have you, or that all this would happen. But here we are."

Akeem found his voice. "How did you do it? I heard you had to learn so much and you somehow passed, but I'm struggling. Did you ever struggle with anything?"

He chuckled. "Oh, I struggled plenty, especially with Ankh techniques and the spiritual side. It felt like I'd never get it. I could fight well, but Kemistry took time. One thing we share is that we learned this when we were much older, which makes it harder to pick up, but you've done so well."

Akeem's voice wavered. "No, I'm not doing so well, especially since the Magi keep telling me I have to fight Muovu soon, and I'm still not sure I can. I'm tired of all the talk. I need something real. I've tried everything, but I keep failing and —"

He paused, feeling a surge of heat from the blazing beacon beside them. King Jabari turned to it. "This is your power."

"My power?" Akeem asked, staring at the light.

"Yes," he murmured. "All those voices in your nightmares were us trying to reach you. And we couldn't reach you until now. The fact that you're here means you tried, and it means you can do this. I'll guide you every step of the way. But we can't stay here long. If you stay too long, you might never come back."

Akeem swallowed hard. "What would happen if I stayed?"

"It's not for living beings to know. Now, you need to go."

As King Jabari spoke, a sudden wind whipped through, and everything blurred. Ashes swirled in the air, and Akeem woke up.

Heart pounding, he jumped up, grabbed a pen, and started writing down everything Jabari had said. Then, he returned to sleep. By the time he awoke, his personal guard entered to help him get dressed, but Akeem barcly noticed. When he finished, he went for breakfast and then met with Kwame for his next lesson.

But this time, they were to take a visit to the Zion temple, which Imani had already told him.

They walked the same path he and Imani had taken the day before and entered the temple. Akeem made sure to act impressed so Kwame wouldn't suspect he'd been there before. This time, they moved deeper until they reached a grand statue that had three faces. It bore the faces of a warrior, a king, and a queen, each crowned in great detail.

Kwame began talking. "This is a sacred site tied to the worship of Nzambi, the Almighty."

"Like your god?" Akeem asked.

"Our God," Kwame corrected. "Every Alkebulan serves the Almighty. No single gender fits; Nzambi embodies balance and harmony; he's a 'he' to men, a 'she' to women, and all that lies between. Nzambi forged the universe using Karbo Kosmic energy — the life force that infuses all living beings, plants, and the cosmos. That's why we revere Him."

"Okay," Akeem whispered, glancing around the dimly lit temple, "so what are we here for? Is this another lesson or something?"

Kwame lifted his head and met Akeem's eyes. "We're here to pray."

Akeem hesitated, shifting on his feet. "Pray? I've never… prayed before."

It was true. Even back in Atlanta, his parents hadn't been religious. They'd never taken him to any service or gathering unless it was for a funeral. And even then, it had felt like going through the motions, not something meaningful. So being asked to pray now was like telling him to ride a beast he'd never even seen before.

Kwame held out a candle, lighting it with one of the already lit candles. He placed it in Akeem's hand and stepped back.

"Just say anything," he murmured. "When you're done, leave the candle."

And then, just like that, Kwame walked away as if Akeem was supposed to know what to do.

Akeem stared at the flame. It flickered, casting shadows on the stone walls. He looked at the carved face of the king. Maybe this was the one he was supposed to pray to. But what was he supposed to say? He didn't even know if he was supposed to close his eyes.

But he did, and let the darkness embrace him.

"I don't know how to do this," he whispered. "I don't know what to say. But if you're out there… please help me. I don't know anything, but I want to learn. I know that when I came here, I was stubborn, like a child. But I don't want to leave without proving I can be better. I'm not that kind of person. So… please help me."

He paused, not sure what else to add. The silence pressed in around him. Even the sounds of the others praying seemed far away, like he was in his own little world.

He opened his eyes and drew in a shaky breath and placed the candle down. Kwame had already finished his prayer and stood a few feet away, waiting. Akeem stepped back, feeling a strange mix of relief and uncertainty. Together, they returned to the sanctuary.

As they entered, they were met by Shabazz at the gate. Akeem tensed, half-expecting a reprimand, but Shabazz only glanced at him, then nodded toward the two figures at his side. Imani stood beside him, but on Shabazz's other side was a tall woman, her posture straight and wearing a black robe that hugged her frame like armor.

Akeem's brow furrowed. "Who's this?"

Shabash gestured to her. "This is Nia. She will be taking you up on etiquette."

"Etiquette?" Akeem repeated. "Even with everything going on, I still have to learn this?"

"It's also important, and Nia is good at it."

Akeem glanced at Nia, noting the way her gaze seemed to assess him in a single sweep. There was no point in arguing. He sighed and nodded. "Alright."

He'd wanted to tell Shabazz about the vision of his father but decided against it with everyone else standing there. Some things needed to be said in private.

They made their way to the dining room, the air heavy with the scent of roasted spices and grilled meats wafting from the kitchen. Shabazz excused himself, leaving Imani by the door.

Akeem felt a little flustered, considering he'd gotten used to Nala always being around him. Now it was Imani. He barely had time to gather his thoughts before a servant arrived, balancing a tray stacked with dishes.

The servant set the tray down, and Nia gestured for Akeem to sit. "Please, start eating," she murmured.

Akeem glanced at her, eyebrows raised. Was she testing him? He hesitated, feeling a little embarrassed—she probably knew he had no etiquette training. But his stomach growled like a restless beast, and he decided to eat, hoping he wouldn't make a fool of himself.

As soon as he picked up his usual spoon, she stopped him. "No," she corrected sharply. "Use the smaller one for the soup. And the larger one for the stew."

For close to an hour, she guided him through every detail: which spoon to use, which hand to hold the fork in, how to sip from a cup without slurping. Akeem thought it was the most exhausting thing he'd done in weeks. All he wanted was to beat Muovu in battle, not learn how to properly hold a spoon.

At one point, she asked him to balance a bowl while taking a sip, and he tried, but it wobbled and nearly spilled. The woman let out an exasperated sigh, pinching the bridge of her nose.

Akeem's face flushed, but before he could say anything, he heard a quiet chuckle from behind. He turned and saw Imani, her eyes bright, though she quickly looked away. But he'd already seen it, and it made him smile.

After the etiquette class ended, he followed the woman out into the hallway. Imani trailed behind him, and he slowed, turning to face her.

"I saw you laugh."

She shook her head, eyes wide. "No, I didn't. Maybe you saw something else," she added, but he wasn't buying it.

"I heard you," he teased, stepping closer. He caught the moment she almost stepped back, but he quickly added, "You looked great, though. I really like seeing that side of you."

Her lips parted, and he caught a flicker of surprise in her expression.

"And... I'm sorry," he continued. "For what I asked at the temple earlier. I didn't mean it like that." Not knowing what to say, he only smiled and then walked ahead, leaving her there.

***

That night, Akeem lay in his bed, thinking of Imani's smile. It reminded him of when he'd first fallen for Zaria and how he'd been captivated by the smallest things—by her laugh, the way her eyes lit up. But this felt different, like a fire smoldering just beneath the surface.

With Zaria, it had felt impossible even from the start—his friends had known it too. Now, thinking about them made his heart tighten. He missed them all so much. Maybe, if he survived this, he'd find a way to see them again.

He sighed and turned his attention back to the books on his desk. He still had so much to learn—about the stones, the techniques, and everything else that had been thrown at him since he'd arrived.

As he read, a sound reached him from outside his window. This time, it wasn't the rustling of leaves or the snap of a branch. He paused as they got clearer. They were voices. He rose and crossed to the window, but the voices were faint.

Curiosity burned through him. He grabbed his jacket and slipped out of the room until he got outside. Turning to his right, he passed a corner and took another, the voices getting clearer now. Just as he crept closer, he recognized the silhouette of Imani standing near the garden wall. She was speaking to someone he couldn't quite see. He couldn't make out what they were saying, but the tone of her voice was serious.

He hesitated. Why was she out here, speaking to someone in the dark?

Not wanting to interrupt them or make it seem like he was following her, he turned and headed back to his room. But his mind didn't still as he wondered what to do.

Not wanting to interrupt them — or make it seem like he was spying — he turned and headed back to his room. But even as he closed the door behind him and reminded himself that it wasn't his business, his mind wouldn't settle.

Maybe he would just ask her if she needed some help. It didn't sound so bad.

CHAPTER 16:

The Ambush

The next morning, Akeem found himself back in etiquette class, forced to listen as Nia droned on about proper spoon usage and table manners. He didn't think this etiquette training was made for him, but he knew that if he could just get through it, he'd move on to something more useful.

He'd hoped to see Imani that morning, but she hadn't come. Maybe she was busy with the royal guard, or maybe she was simply avoiding him after the awkwardness the night before. He didn't even know what he'd say if he did see her — whether to bring up what he saw or pretend like he knew nothing.

He pushed those thoughts away just as the connecting door to the kitchen area finally swung open and servants began bringing in platters. Akeem sighed with relief, his stomach growling. Just then, as he turned to glance at the food, he felt a light brush against his leg. He looked down, surprised to see Nala slipping a folded paper into his pocket before vanishing as quickly as she'd appeared.

His heart leapt. He hadn't seen Nala in ages. Shabazz hadn't mentioned anything about her new assignment — maybe he'd thought Akeem would go searching for her. Well, now that she'd come to him — dressed like the kitchen staff — he couldn't pretend he didn't see her.

When he finished eating, he stepped out of the dining room. He pulled the paper from his pocket and read her hurried scrawl: Please, my lord, come to the kitchen area, but outside, not inside. There is something important I need to tell you.

She needed to tell him something? He'd expected her to just say hello, but now, he was just curious and half-worried too.

Also, he had wanted to speak to her and apologize for how things turned out. With that, he made his way outside — half-wondering where Imani was, following the scent of spices until he reached the kitchen's side entrance.

This was the same side where he'd seen Imani speaking to that shadowy figure the night before. He frowned, feeling suspicious. Had Nala seen something she wasn't supposed to?

He wished he had seen Imani and asked, but remembering her reaction at the temple, he hesitated. She'd seemed so sensitive about her love life, and he didn't want to make her feel like he was prying. He exhaled silently. And maybe Nala saw nothing, too. He hoped so.

Just as he turned a corner, he heard a sudden scuffling sound like someone running toward him. Before he could react, a glint of steel suddenly flashed, coming at him fast. Instinct screamed, and he twisted sideways, the blade slicing through the air just inches from his face.

He dropped low, his mind snapping into overdrive, the lessons from his basic combat training flooding back. No staff this time. He'd have to rely on his body and reflexes. He ducked another swipe.

His attacker lunged again, and Akeem turned, sweeping a leg. The move threw the attacker off balance for a second — enough time for Akeem to throw a punch at the figure's midsection. It landed hard, but the attacker barely flinched, only grunting beneath a dark hood.

Akeem felt pain in his arm as the attacker's blade grazed him. He hissed but didn't let it affect his focus. He grabbed a handful of dirt from the ground and flung it toward the attacker's eyes, which was a failure in hindsight, but the figure batted it away with a gloved hand.

The attacker lunged again, and Akeem had no choice but to grab at the face, his fingers curling into the hood, yanking it down. And there, beneath the mask, eyes wide with shock, was Nala.

"Nala?" he gasped.

At that moment, he heard his name from behind.

"Prince Akeem!"

He turned his head just as Imani appeared, her own blade drawn, eyes hard with fury.

Nala, now covering her face with the remaining pieces of her mask, tried to slip free, but Imani lunged, blocking her path. The two women faced off, blades flashing.

Akeem's mind spun. "Imani, wait—"

He lunged forward to grab Imani's arm, but she jerked away, her eyes wide in shock. Akeem barely had time to react as Nala's blade sliced through the air and into his upper arm.

Immediately, blood splashed across his sleeve and dripped down his fingers. He staggered back, clutching the wound.

Nala's eyes flickered with something he couldn't name—fear, maybe, or triumph—before she ran, disappearing into the maze of corridors.

Imani spun toward him, her eyes wild. "Prince Akeem!" she cried, catching him as he swayed.

Other guards burst into the courtyard, weapons drawn, eyes scanning for the threat.

"Find her!" someone yelled, but Nala was already gone.

Akeem clutched his bleeding arm, hot blood seeping through his fingers. He gritted his teeth as pain thundered up his side and everything in sight spun.

"Prince Akeem!" Imani's voice cut through the haze. She was at his side, eyes wide with panic. "Stay with me!" Imani's voice cut through the haze. "You're bleeding—"

"It's nothing," he lied, trying to smile, but it came with pain.

"Medic! Get him on the stretcher now!" Someone barked, and two guards hoisted him up, placing him gently onto a stretcher. Akeem's vision blurred as he struggled to stay conscious.

Shabazz appeared, his eyes scanning the blood on Akeem's clothes. "What happened?"

Akeem's lips moved, but the words caught in his throat. Nala's face flashed before his eyes—eyes filled with something he couldn't name. Was it guilt? Fear?

"It—it was too fast," he forced out. "I couldn't see who it was."

Shabazz's eyes narrowed, searching Akeem's face for the truth. "It seems to be an assassination attempt," he muttered, more to himself than anyone else. "Muovu knows you're alive."

Akeem's pulse skittered, his head pounding. Muovu? Could Nala be working with him? His thoughts tangled like a mass of thorns, every question sharper than the last.

A sudden movement caught his eye, and Imani's face came into view, though it swam and blurred. She looked pale.

Shabazz's gaze darted to her. "Where were you when this happened?" he snapped. "You were supposed to be watching him—"

"I was with him! I tried to stop it—I almost got hit myself!"

"You let him get ambushed in the sanctuary," Shabazz countered.

"I didn't let anything happen!" She shot back.

Akeem tried to lift his head, to speak, but his lips parted and no words came. The pain rushed in like a tide, dragging him under. He reached for Shabazz's sleeve, but his strength gave out.

"Wait," he whispered, but the darkness swallowed his words. The last thing he felt was someone's hand tightening on his shoulder as the world slipped away.

***

When he opened his eyes again, Akeem knew instantly that he was back in his dream. This time, there was no one on his left. But to his right, a figure waited—a tall woman with skin like polished obsidian and eyes that shone like moonlight.

"Mother?" he whispered, his breath catching.

Queen Malaika's face was wet with tears, her beauty undimmed by the sorrow in her eyes. She wore a flowing indigo robe and just like his father, a crown rested on her head.

"Akeem," she murmured, her voice trembling. "My son, I've missed you so much." She reached out her hand, and he reached forward to her, his hands grasping hers, small and warm.

"Mother..." he murmured, his voice breaking. He fell into her embrace, feeling her arms wrap around him.

When they separated, he felt the need to pour out everything.

"Mother, I... I made a mistake. I thought I was doing the right thing, but I think I hurt someone." His voice faltered. "I trusted too much. I thought everyone around me wanted to see Muovu fall. But it seems... it seems there was someone who didn't. And now—now I feel like I'm the one who let everyone down."

Queen Malaika's expression softened as she brushed a thumb over his cheek. "Akeem, don't blame yourself for trusting others. Trust is a gift and a reflection of the goodness in your own heart. When others betray that trust, it shows their failings, not yours." She paused. "It is not wrong to trust people. It is wrong for them to break that trust."

"But what am I supposed to do now? Shabazz will have questions. I don't even know how to face him. How am I supposed to stand against someone who's been helping me? I don't know who to trust anymore. Nala — she tried to kill me. She —" He glanced down at his arm but found no wound there.

Queen Malaika cupped his face in her hands, returning his gaze to her. "My son," she murmured, "listen to your heart, and learn to listen well. Look for the patterns between the words; only then will you find the truth. And remember: your strength is not just in your sword or your staff, but in your spirit and your mind."

"But what if I choose wrong?" he whispered.

She smiled softly. "Then you will learn. Every choice teaches us, even the hard ones. You will rise, Akeem. You are stronger than you know."

Her voice began to fade, the mist curling around her. Akeem reached for her, but her touch slipped away, leaving only the scent of jasmine lingering in the air.

"Wake now, my son," she murmured. "Wake and be ready."

Akeem gasped and opened his eyes, the dawn light breaking across his face.

CHAPTER 17:

Training

Akeem blinked up at the white ceiling. The sterile scent was a tell that he was in the sick bay. A soft sound made him turn his head. There, to his right, sat Imani in a cushioned chair, her head tilted to the side, resting against the armrest. She was asleep.

Her face was peaceful and still, her long lashes brushing her cheeks. It was strange how different she looked in sleep. Softer and unburdened. A single braid had come undone, curling near her cheek. Almost without thinking, Akeem reached out to brush it back. His fingers barely grazed the strand when her eyes opened.

They stared at each other.

His hand jerked back, pain shooting up his arm. He winced, and Imani sat up fast.

"Are you all right?"

He forced a smile. "I'm good. Just a little pain."

She wasn't convinced. Without asking, she reached for his left arm, moving closer as she examined the bandages. Her shadow fell over him, and for a moment, he forgot how to breathe.

"Okay," she murmured softly, letting his arm go. "You look better."

Akeem tried to hide the rush of heat in his face. He grinned, hoping to ease the tension. "What would you have done if I weren't?"

Her expression soured instantly. "I'd have done my job," she murmured flatly. "Same as before, if you'd let me. Why did you stop me?"

He hesitated, licking his lips. "I didn't want you to get hurt."

"I wouldn't have," she murmured, her tone tightening. "It's my job to keep you safe, Prince Akeem. You shouldn't have stepped in."

It felt like getting scolded by a mother, and part of him was even glad for it. But he also felt small, like she still saw him as a boy.

He shifted to sit up. Imani leaned in, maybe to help, but he raised a hand, and she waited while he pushed himself upright. The pain in his arm was still there, but numbed by whatever the nurses had given him.

When he finally faced her, he met her eyes fully.

"I know I reacted too fast, but at that moment… it felt like I had to. It was either me or you."

"The blade was meant for me, not you. And now I've failed. Someone got to you under my watch. I'm going to make sure that intruder is punished—"

"She wasn't caught?" Akeem asked, a bit too quickly.

Imani narrowed her eyes. "You know the person?"

His mouth opened; he hadn't meant to say that. She didn't see Nala's face. And if she found out who it was…he didn't want to imagine her reaction.

"I just assumed," he murmured, trying to sound casual. "I didn't see anything. I swear."

Imani stared at him. "If you saw something, you have to tell me."

"I didn't," Akeem said. "Just assumed. Don't worry." He pivoted quickly. "I heard Shabazz was blaming you. I'm sorry about that."

She shook her head. "It's my fault. I should've checked whether you had your guard with you. If you didn't, I should've been there myself." She paused, then tilted her head. "But why were you even going to the kitchen area? I didn't think you even knew that entrance."

The question he'd been dreading. Of course, Imani would ask. She was too sharp not to.

"I just wanted to see what it looked like," he murmured, shrugging.

"Really?" Her tone sharpened. "Because the connecting door takes you right into the kitchen. Easiest way in. Almost like someone led you there."

"Does it matter?" Akeem asked, meeting her gaze, only to regret it instantly. She didn't believe him. "I just needed some air," he added quickly. "I'm sorry for not saying anything."

Imani reached into her pocket and pulled out a folded piece of paper.

"We found this," she murmured.

Akeem's stomach dropped.

She unfolded it slowly. "Someone gave you this. Asking you to meet them there." She looked up. "Who is she?"

Akeem's hands flew to his pockets, already knowing the note was gone. There it was, right in Imani's grip.

He swallowed hard.

"W-what? It's no one—"

"Prince Akeem," she snapped, dragging the chair closer to his bed. "This is important. I can't stress it enough. Someone attacked you—"

"It's not the person who gave me the paper!" he burst out, louder than intended. He stopped himself before he murmured too much. Two thoughts warred in his head: Nala attacked him, but... why? "Nala wanted to talk," he muttered.

"So... You didn't see who attacked you?" Imani leaned back slightly.

"No," he murmured, voice lower. "But it wasn't Nala."

There was silence. Then a slow exhale from Imani. "You seem to trust her a lot but—"

"Well, I trusted you," he cut in, "and you haven't killed me yet. I think I'm fine."

Her eyes narrowed.

"Why would Nala attack me?" He pressed. "Can't you see that none of it makes sense?"

She didn't answer that. Instead, she asked quietly, "Do you like her?"

His breath caught. "W-what?" He sputtered. "What are you talking about?"

"I guess from your answer, it's true." Her face changed, the earlier warmth draining out. "It's against the rule," she murmured, voice suddenly flat, "for a royal and a guard to fall in love."

"I'm not in love with her!"

The outburst made her flinch. He immediately regretted it. His next words were softer.

"I'm not in love with Nala," he murmured again. "She was my first guard and made me feel less alone. That's all. She's a friend. Nothing more."

He wasn't sure she believed him at first, but slowly her expression eased.

"Oh," she murmured quietly. "I thought…"

"No. I'm only saying all this because… I need to understand what's happening. That's all."

She was quiet for a beat. Then: "We got her."

"You got who?"

Imani shifted, looking a bit uneasy. "I lied to you. We already have her. She was trying to change clothes, but the guards got her just in time."

Akeem's heart sank. "You—why didn't you tell me?"

"You were so concerned," she murmured, avoiding his eyes. "I wanted to see if there was more you'd say. Also… I thought you were romantically involved with her. I needed to be careful."

Her voice cracked at the end, and Akeem stopped himself from reacting. He had questions—so many — but they could wait. Nala was in custody. He didn't know what Shabazz would do. That scared him more than the blade had.

"I need to see her," he murmured, already pulling back the covers. He noticed his clothes had been changed, hopefully not by Imani.

"I'm sorry, you can't," she murmured, rising to her feet. "We'll question her. We'll get the answers—"

"I just want to see her. That's all."

She shook her head.

"Is there a rule," he asked, voice hardening, "that says a royal can't see a prisoner?"

"If the prisoner is dangerous," she murmured, meeting his eyes, "then no, you can't."

He stood, pain buzzing in his arm, but it did not stop him. Now he was eye-to-eye with her.

"And if I have a guard who will do everything to keep me safe?"

She swallowed. "Y-you can go," she murmured quietly.

"Good." He stepped back. "You keep reminding me to act like a leader. Well… I think it's time I did."

Her lips thinned at that. She didn't like it. He saw it in her eyes, and again, he regretted the words. But he couldn't take them back. Not now.

Imani bowed slightly. "Okay, my lord. Please follow me."

She turned, and Akeem followed. The sick bay was in another wing of the building, closer to the jails. After two quick turns, they reached a narrow hallway. At the end was a door, which Imani pushed open.

There were five cells barricaded by steel bars, and inside was a bed and a toilet. That was all. Nala was in the second. She looked up and froze.

"Prince Akeem!" She cried, rushing to the bars, eyes wide with desperation. "Please, help me!"

Akeem stepped forward, but Imani caught his arm.

"You can't get too close," she murmured. "Just a few meters. Please, for your safety."

He hesitated, then nodded. "Alright."

He walked until he was close, but not close enough to reach through the bars. He didn't think Nala would hurt him. Not with Imani here. Still…

"I'm so glad you're alive, my lord," Nala said, voice cracking as tears welled in her eyes. "I didn't mean to do it…"

"Then why did you?"

"I didn't mean to," she murmured again, sniffling. "I was f-forced."

Akeem stepped closer. Imani made a warning sound behind him, but he didn't stop.

"Who forced you?"

He already knew what she was about to say.

"My family…" Her voice trembled. "Muovu took my family. When I got home, they were gone, and there was a letter there. It said if I just… did it, they'd be brought back."

He didn't need to ask what they asked her to do. "You didn't tell anyone?"

She shook her head violently. "I couldn't. They said they'd kill them. I didn't know what to do. I was so scared. If Muovu got hold of them, I'd never see them again... I thought if I just—" Her voice cracked. "I thought it'd be over quickly. That they'd let them go."

"You didn't know what else to do," Akeem said quietly.

She nodded, tears streaming freely. "Please. I didn't want to hurt you. But he took my family..."

And Akeem believed her. That's what he'd needed to understand. He remembered the fear in her eyes, even as she raised the blade. Something had always felt... off.

"Okay," he murmured. "I'll see what I can do."

She wiped her eyes and stretched out a trembling hand. He took it, ignoring Imani's sharp gasp behind him. Her hand was small and slick with sweat, and he squeezed it once before letting go. Without a word, he turned away. Imani followed, silent.

As they walked back through the hall, he could feel her wanting to speak, but she murmured nothing. Not until they reached Shabazz's door.

Just as his hand touched the knob, a voice behind them:

"I assume you've already seen Nala?"

They turned. Shabazz stood in the corridor, watching.

Akeem straightened. "She murmured Muovu took her family."

"She told us the same."

"And what are you doing about it?"

Shabazz tilted his head. "We're taking precautions."

"Precautions?" Akeem almost snapped. "One of your guards had her entire family taken. Isn't the next step to get them out?"

"And should I do the same for the ten thousand others Muovu has taken?" Shabazz asked.

Silence fell between them.

"You're not going to help her?" Akeem asked slowly.

"If that's all you gathered from this conversation," Shabazz said, "then maybe we shouldn't be having it."

Akeem's jaw clenched. "Then what's the point of being a prince if I can't save someone's family? Not just anyone—my guard. My personal aide."

Shabazz sighed. "That's not what I meant. But we can't rush into this. I won't send an army charging into Muovu's territory. If I do, this place is left vulnerable. You're not ready to face him, and if he gets the stones, he won't just kill you. He'll kill everyone."

Akeem heard the logic, but the truth stung.

"So… we sacrifice a few to save the many?"

Shabazz looked at him long and hard, weighing the words. Then:

"What I'm saying is you need to think. I know you care about her. We all do. But look at the full picture. She still came here to kill you. She didn't tell us anything. She could've warned someone, and she didn't. What if Imani hadn't stopped her? What if we hadn't caught her?"

He stepped forward.

"She would've struck again. And this time, she wouldn't have missed."

Akeem said nothing.

"So," Shabazz finished, voice low, "I hope you understand why I'm asking you to think clearly. Not with your heart."

He heard every word, and still something inside him refused to settle. He wanted to tear a hole in that reasoning, but the truth was, Shabazz was right. He knew it. He just didn't want to.

"So, what happens now?" Akeem asked, voice quieter than he meant. "What are you going to do with her?"

"We'll investigate," Shabazz said, watching him closely. "And I promise you that it would be fair."

Akeem nodded, but before he could speak again, Shabazz was already moving forward.

"But you need to focus," he murmured. "Your training has to become your only priority."

Akeem's brow furrowed. "I've been learning. I've been reading everything I can find on the Alkeic stones, on how they work and what they respond to. I just started sparring again—"

"That's where you stay," Shabazz cut in, but with an edge now. "Sparring. Fighting. Strength. That is what matters right now." He turned to Imani. "Cancel every other lesson. Martial arts only. I want him ready. We move on to Muovu soon."

Then he looked back at Akeem, and something about his stance felt heavier than before.

"I know it feels fast, and maybe it is, but this attempt on your life means Muovu knows you're here, and if he knows, he is already preparing. We do not have time to breathe."

Akeem swallowed hard. He understood, and yet some part of him wished it hadn't taken Nala's betrayal to open their eyes. He wished they had seen the storm before the first drop of blood.

But now, it was too late to wish.

CHAPTER 18:

Power and Possibilities

One thing Akeem had always been drawn to, long before he ever knew what fate had planned for him, was technology. Beyond the games and toys, there was something that made him ask questions no one around him had the patience to answer. He wanted to know how things worked, how light bulbs glowed, how gadgets came alive when connected to the wall.

His curiosity wasn't passive. He tore things apart, dismantling radios, remote controls, and toasters just to see what lay hidden inside. His parents had tried, at first, to stop him, scolding him when he left appliances gutted, but it was useless. He wasn't trying to destroy; he was trying to understand.

One summer, he picked up odd jobs around the neighborhood—mowing lawns, cleaning garages, doing anything that could earn him a few extra dollars—but even then, the things he wanted were far beyond what his earnings could reach. So he went to his father, explained that he wanted the broken ones they no longer used, and his father agreed. For the first time, Akeem had his own little lab of discarded electronics, each one waiting for resurrection.

They weren't glamorous. Most were too old, too outdated to be exciting, but for a boy who wanted to learn, they were gold. And then he got the computer.

At first, he used it the way most kids did, browsing, playing games, watching videos, but then he saw a spy film—one of those fast-paced stories where the hero hacked into a government server in less than five minutes—and it sparked something in him. That night, he typed "how to hack" into the search bar, and that was where it all began.

What he found wasn't like the movies. It wasn't quick. It was messy and technical and required time, skill, and patience. And more than that, it was dangerous. His parents hadn't known at first, but when he mentioned what he was trying to learn, the look in his father's eyes was different. He had threatened to take the computer away entirely, and Akeem, confused and angry, hadn't understood why.

Now, looking back, he thought maybe they had been afraid of Muovu even then, afraid their son's brilliance would become bait, or worse, a weapon in the wrong hands. But he hadn't seen it that way. Back then, he'd just thought they were paranoid and unwilling to believe that the world had changed.

So, he kept going.

He found corners of the internet that weren't meant to be found, and he lingered there. The dark web wasn't just something you stumbled into—it took months, even years, to understand how to access it safely and to understand what kind of fire you were playing with. He never bought anything, never engaged directly, but he saw enough to know how deep the rabbit hole went.

When it came time to choose a path for college, he didn't hesitate. Computer programming and cybersecurity. The words looked clean, and they erased the nervous edge in his parents' eyes whenever they heard him speak. Now, he wasn't trying to be a hacker; he was training to be a future IT professional.

But that wasn't the truth.

That course was his gateway. The deeper he went into the curriculum, the more he realized how much of it overlapped with the skills he had already begun to teach himself—network penetration, system vulnerabilities, encryption and code injection.

He began testing himself more and more. Small things, harmless things, or so he convinced himself—cracking admin passwords, slipping into restricted school systems, adjusting a grade or two, but only his own, never for others or profit. It was about control.

And control was intoxicating.

When he breached a local bank's firewall, just to see if he could, his heart had pounded so loud he thought the walls would hear it. He didn't take a dime and he left no trace. But the fact that he could was enough to light something electric in his chest.

But no matter how many systems he cracked, it never felt like enough.

Then came the job offer—junior security analyst at CyberFort Solutions, one of the country's top tech firms. His parents were thrilled. But just as

he was settling into the idea, Alkebulan happened.

And that changed everything.

There was power inside the Alkeic stones, and for
the first time, Akeem understood what he could
really do there.

Rising from his seat, he grabbed his journal and
stepped out of the room with Imani close behind
him. It had been four days since the attempt on
his life—though he hated calling it that—and
ever since, he'd resumed sparring with Imani,
who had taken Shabazz's warning seriously. He
could feel the intensity behind her strikes and the
way she never quite softened, even when they
laughed between sessions. There was tension in
the air between them, in the way their hands
brushed, and in the things they hadn't said since
Nala's confession.

He hadn't figured out how to bring it up without
sounding strange or reckless. And there were
moments when he caught her looking at him a
second longer than necessary. He remembered
what she'd said before, about the royal family
and forbidden ties, and it lingered in his chest.
But his parents had done it.

Still, now wasn't the time to talk about that.

He stopped in front of Shabazz's door and stepped inside. The older man was already standing, looking like he had been on his way out, but Akeem didn't wait.

"I know how we can use the Alkeic stones," he murmured, slamming the journal onto the table with more force than intended.

Shabazz's brow lifted. "What's the idea?"

"We embed the stones into armor," Akeem said. "They're indestructible, and they boost tech. If we fuse them into gear—armor, weapons, anything—they could amplify our defense and enhance energy output. Think about it. That's how we get an edge."

"So, you mean using them to strengthen physical ability?"

"Exactly. They already react to us. So why not harness it?"

Imani stepped forward. "The Magi tried things like this before, but it was unstable. What if the integration fractures? What if the energy pushes back? We don't even fully understand how they work yet."

Shabazz nodded. "She's right. There's still so much we don't know about the stones, especially when it comes to channeling them into physical constructs. If something goes wrong, it won't just fail; it could destroy the person wearing it."

Akeem nodded, but his eyes didn't waver. "Fair. But here's the thing—you all worked with raw energy and no systems to regulate flow. My world is systems. Coding, security, fail-safes. I can design a stabilizer that bridges the stone's power to tech without the chaos."

Shabazz rubbed his chin, gaze narrowing. "You really think you can pull that off? No offense, Prince Akeem, but this is different from anything you've ever seen—"

"Energy is energy," Akeem cut in. "Whether it's a current or a force buried in stones. It still follows rules. I just need time."

Shabazz exhaled slowly, but a faint smile curved his lips. "Alright. Say we agreed. What's your first move?"

"Testing with one stone," Akeem replied. "We watch how it reacts, how much it gives, and how far it reaches. If it holds, we build on it."

For a few moments, Shabazz seemed to think and then nodded.

"When you're ready, I'll go with you to the tech center."

Akeem smiled then. "Thank you."

He turned, and just before he stepped out, Imani caught his gaze. She gave a quick smile, and Akeem returned it. In that look, he made up his mind.

He would make it work. For himself and for them.

***

The wooden staffs were gone. They had moved past that now.

Real swords moved in their hands, dulled at the edge but still metal. Akeem had grown sharper. He no longer stumbled, no longer hesitated and simply flowed. He parried and struck with enough precision to make Imani raise one brow in approval.

He had begun seeing light again. Not the brilliant glow that wrapped around Imani, but something subtler. At night, he also trained — breath control and the rituals — and it felt like he was becoming one with them.

Now, under the afternoon sun, they danced across the training yard, blades crashing. Imani was still faster but he was keeping pace now, and that mattered.

Suddenly, their swords locked mid-strike. They were close. Too close. Breath tangled with breath, sweat catching the sunlight on their skin. Akeem's heartbeat slammed in his chest. Neither moved. For one long second, the world held its breath.

Then Akeem leaned in.

Imani's eyes widened. And for a second, she didn't pull back. She lingered there, lips parted like she'd forgotten to breathe. But then something flickered behind her eyes, and she stepped away.

Akeem did the same.

"Sorry —"

They both said it at the same time. Akeem let out a breath, half a laugh, shaking his head. Imani smiled too.

Akeem gestured toward her. "You first."

She hesitated, gripping her sword a little too tightly, then twirled it. "Um... just wanted to say you're getting better."

That wasn't what she'd meant to say. They both knew it. Whatever had hovered at the edge of her lips had vanished the moment silence broke. It was nerves, maybe, or timing. But she'd swallowed it and that made it easier for Akeem to follow her lead.

"Still not on your level," he murmured, the corner of his mouth lifting. "But... thank you for everything."

"It's all for the cause," she replied, with a smile.

And just like that, something between them gave way. It wasn't everything, not yet. But the wall they'd built had finally cracked. Akeem could feel it. And he hoped he'd be the one to break it down completely.

***

That night, for the first time in a long while, Akeem slept without dreams.

CHAPTER 19:

The Garden

Since the day they began sparring, Akeem had been watching Imani—not just her speed or strength, but the cracks. She was fast, nearly impossible to land a strike on, but she wasn't perfect. He'd seen the subtle tells: how she slightly favored her left side after a high strike, how she hesitated before a feint, and how there was always the smallest pause before a counter.

They were small, but enough.

Today, under the sharp sun, sweat already lining his brow, he decided to test the theory. Their sparring had been relentless, but Akeem held on patiently, waiting for that moment.

And then it did. She swung high, blade arcing toward his shoulder. He blocked. He saw the opening. And he took it.

His sword slipped past her guard, the blunt edge tapping against her ribs. Silence fell like a curtain.

Imani froze, and then her sword lowered. Her dark eyes, wide with disbelief, locked onto his.

"You—"

Akeem stepped back, a grin spreading across his face. "Got you."

He waited for the scowl. Her pride was sharp, and he'd just punctured it. But then, she laughed while shaking her head in surprise.

"Took you long enough," she murmured. There was something new in her gaze now. He couldn't name it exactly, but it wasn't mockery. Not annoyance. Something else.

He wiped the sweat from his face and turned to leave the training yard with the win pulsing in his veins.

"Prince Akeem."

He turned back.

She looked almost shy as she asked, "Would you like to go somewhere with me?"

He blinked. "Are we going to the temple?"

"No," she murmured, smiling. "Somewhere better."

He didn't hesitate as curiosity tugged at him. And truthfully, he just wanted more time with her.

She led him away from the yard, past stone courtyards and fountains, deeper into the palace compound. He hadn't walked this path before. Vines with violet blossoms curled around carved archways. The air grew cooler.

Then they reached it. It was a garden.

It was hidden behind a wall of trees, and the grass was soft, and the flowers bloomed in colors he didn't even have names for. Birds flitted between branches, singing as they did.

"What is this place?" he asked, stunned. "Why didn't I know it was here?"

"Welcome to the Garden of Eternal Spring," Imani said, stepping lightly onto a stone path. "My retreat."

Akeem blinked. "You have your own garden?"

"Not officially," she murmured with a smirk. "Most people don't come out this far, so I claimed it."

He laughed. "Is this where you come after training?"

She gave a slow smile, eyes half-lidded. That was answer enough.

He looked around again. Everything about this place—the stillness, the colors, the way the sunlight spilled through the branches—made it make sense that she would belong here.

"Why bring me?" he asked.

She didn't answer right away. Instead, she crouched beside a curling stream, dragging her fingers through the cool water. Then, softly, she spoke. "This place... it's peace. It reminds me of everything we're trying to protect. I brought you here so you could just... breathe. Let the world pause for a moment."

They wandered through the garden, the vibrant hues of the flowers creating a kaleidoscope of colors around them. Eventually, they reached the edge of the garden, where the sound of rushing water grew louder. Imani led Akeem down a narrow path, and soon, they stood before a waterfall Imani called "Mrembo Falls." The waterfall cascaded down from a towering cliff, its waters glistening in the sunlight before plunging into a crystal-clear pool below. The air was cool and refreshing, the mist from the falls enveloping them in a fine spray.

"Isn't it beautiful?" Imani asked, her eyes shining with excitement.

Akeem could only nod, captivated by the sight before him.

And then, as if letting go of a thought she'd carried too long, she turned to him. "You've changed," she murmured softly. "You're not the man who stumbled through his first spar anymore."

She didn't say it with judgment. She murmured it with wonder.

Akeem tilted his head. "And that's… good?"

She stood, looking straight at him. "It's interesting."

There was a beat of silence.

"You've been practicing a lot," she murmured.

"How did you—?"

"I've trained a lot of people. None of them got better like you. And the lights around you are getting brighter."

He didn't know what to say. He didn't even know how to breathe for a moment. Imani praised him.

Then she turned without a word and walked ahead. She passed the waterfall, its roar softening behind them, until they reached a bed of wildflowers blanketing the earth. She crouched and plucked a crimson bloom from a low bush, holding it between her fingers.

"You won today," she murmured, eyes on the flower, "because you paid attention. Most don't. They watch me fight and see someone they think can't be touched. But they never look close enough."

Akeem watched her, watched the way the sun caught on the beads threaded through her braids. The garden framed her like a painting.

"Everyone has weaknesses," he murmured, voice quiet now.

It was rare to see her like this, and he didn't want the moment to slip away.

"Even you?" she asked.

"Especially me," he answered.

Then, without warning, she extended the flower toward him, her smirk returning. "Don't let it go to your head. I'm still going to wipe the floor with you tomorrow."

He took the flower, fingers brushing hers, a grin blooming across his face. "Looking forward to it."

But the shift came fast, and he felt it before she even said a word. Her eyes dropped, her hands found the hem of her tunic, fingers pulled at it. Then she inhaled slowly and spoke.

"Prince Akeem... I need to apologize."

He opened his mouth to respond, but she didn't let him.

"For how I treated you when you first got here," she continued, her voice softer now. "The things I said and the way I acted. I was harsh and wasn't fair to you."

He looked at her, surprised, the flower still resting in his hand like he had forgotten he was holding it.

"It's alright," he murmured after a breath. "I wasn't exactly easy to deal with, and... you were right. I had a lot of growing up to do. I wasn't ready to lead anyone back then."

"Still. I could have been kinder."

He chuckled and shook his head. "By the way, did you really hate me back then?"

"No," she murmured a little too fast.

He raised an eyebrow. "That wasn't convincing."

She rolled her eyes. "Fine. I thought you were stuck-up. And you complained a lot."

"Wow." He pressed a hand to his chest, faking offense. "And here I was thinking I was charming."

"You were insufferable."

They laughed, and it felt good, like something long buried had finally been shaken loose. But then his tone shifted as he looked at her again.

"And what do you think of me now?"

She stilled, her expression unreadable for a moment as her eyes searched his. Then she murmured it.

"I think you're doing well. And... I'm proud of you."

The words hit him hard. They settled in his chest like something he had been waiting for.

He swallowed, fingers curling tighter around the flower. "I... I'll do everything right," he murmured. "I won't let you down. I mean, Alkebulan. All of it."

"I see that, and I'll stay by your side to help."

That made something flutter in him.

So, of course, he smirked. "So... does this mean you finally believe me about Nala?"

Imani stiffened almost imperceptibly. "That's not my business, and I apologise if —"

"No," he murmured, stepping closer. "But since we're clearing the air, let's clear that too. There's nothing between us. There never was. And I'm not hiding anything."

She looked at him long and hard until finally she gave a quiet sigh. "Okay."

He tilted his head. "Okay?"

"Okay."

He nodded. And then, because he had always been terrible at leaving things where they belonged, he asked, "So... who was that person you were talking to that night?"

Imani's eyes flew wide. "What?"

"You know," he murmured. "That night by the kitchen corridor. I heard voices."

She blinked at him, somewhere between shock and disbelief. "You were spying on me?"

"Not spying," he murmured, lifting his hands. "It was late and I heard voices. You're the one who told me to watch for suspicious activity, so I did. Turned out it was you."

For a second, he thought she might walk away, but instead she laughed.

"You're impossible."

"And you're avoiding the question," he replied, noticing she had dropped all formality without realizing it. He didn't point it out.

She shook her head, but her voice was soft now. "It was nothing. Just... family matters."

Akeem arched a brow. "Family that made you look like you were ready to set something on fire?"

Her gaze slipped to the stream. "It's complicated."

He waited.

After a long breath, she murmured, "You've met my brother, Akili, but not everyone knows. I've kept it quiet for his safety..."

That name coiled in Akeem's spine. Muovu, the butcher of their past and the monster who tore families apart.

"He's all I have left," she went on. "And he wants to go to the city and see it for himself, but I told him no. He's brilliant, but if Muovu ever found out about it—"

"He won't," Akeem said. "I'll make sure of it. Muovu won't get close."

She looked at him, and after a beat, she smiled. "Thank you."

Akeem nudged her shoulder. "So, if Akili's your brother, does that mean I get to tease him? Ask him all kinds of embarrassing questions about you?"

She actually giggled, and he laughed too, and for a moment it felt like nothing outside the garden could touch them.

Then, because he could never leave well enough alone, he murmured, "You know, I thought maybe he was your... you know, your lover. I felt guilty eavesdropping. But... have you ever thought about marriage?"

She raised a brow. "That's your follow-up?"

"Just curious."

She plucked a leaf from the branch beside her, turned it in her fingers, voice distant. "I had someone. A long time ago. But royal guards don't really have time for love."

"You said they also can't—"

"Be in love with royalty," she finished. "It's forbidden."

Akeem's voice was quiet now, like it barely made it through his lips. "And that applies to you, too?"

She didn't answer right away. When she did, her voice was low.

"Yes. Duty comes first."

"Still. Seems like a lonely way to live."

Imani held his gaze, unreadable. "It is what it is."

The silence that followed wasn't cold. It settled between them, as if one of them had left something unsaid and the other was waiting to catch it.

Then Imani sighed and smiled. "We should head back. You need to freshen up."

Only then did he remember the sweat drying on his skin. He almost sniffed himself but thought better of it. They walked back side by side, and just before parting ways, her smile stayed with him, burning into his memory.

***

By day, Akeem sparred. By night, he worked.

He had a plan. A different plan from what he told Shabazz and Imani. A reckless, brilliant plan. One that needed him to slip into places he had no permission to be. But if it worked, Alkebulan would never fall.

First, he went to the tech center, found Akili, and asked harmless questions about the defense network. Told him he just wanted to understand it better. Akili was so glad to see him that he barely asked why.

Four nights later, the victory was his.

But it hadn't come easily. Each night, Akeem had sat at the interface, entering the access codes Akili had unknowingly given him. The system fought back—firewalls flaring red, protocols locking down one after the other—but he kept going, slipping through the cracks. Until finally, he broke through.

He reached the core.

The command nexus where every ship, turret, drone, and array should have been connected, was separated. Each system drifting like an island.

Akeem could change that.

His fingers flew, rewriting code and weaving broken systems together. Sweat tracked down his brow as the interface pulsed with warnings. But he didn't flinch and pushed deeper.

One final keystroke. The screen glitched and then held. A green light blinked.

SYSTEMS SYNCHRONIZED.

His breath caught. It had worked.

Every weapon, every defense in Alkebulan now spoke with one voice. No gaps. No lag. If an enemy moved, the entire grid would move with it. A laugh tore out of him.

"Yes!"

He'd done it.

CHAPTER 20:

Warning

Shabazz kept his word.

When Akeem finally felt ready to explain the idea, they went together to the tech center with Imani and the two Magi who had shown too much interest to be left out. Akili was already there and, like before, raised the same concerns as Shabazz and Imani. Still, they agreed to try again.

What surprised Akeem most was how quickly they began. He'd expected hesitation. But instead, the team got to work.

He didn't know the practical applications of the stones, only what he had read, and even that was a patchwork of theory. So, he wrote everything down, especially what to do if it failed. He wanted to stay, but Shabazz reminded him that the tech center was there to serve, and Akeem's part was the vision, not the labor. If they needed him, they'd call.

It wasn't that he didn't trust them, though in truth, he barely knew any of them, but he wanted to witness it. But he decided to learn to trust. Besides, it gave him more time with Imani.

Ever since that day, the air between them had lightened. The stiffness was gone, replaced by banter. Still, Akeem could feel her holding something back. He hadn't forgotten what she murmured about love being forbidden for the royal guard.

She'd even been engaged once. That alone told him how close she'd come to living a life she walked away from. It made him wonder every time they sparred. It distracted him.

"Prince Akeem?"

He blinked, sword lowered, the world rushing back in. Imani was watching him, concern in her gaze.

"You alright?"

He gave a quick smile, not ready to share what sat in his chest. "Just thinking. I'm fine."

She didn't look convinced, but she murmured nothing, only reset her stance, blade raised. He mirrored her, and this time, she struck first. He dodged. She'd grown more defensive since he found her weaknesses, but he'd been careful not to exploit them. Still, he won sometimes.

He liked sparring with her. Liked how the lights danced as they moved. With every clash of blades, he was beginning to understand them more. Also, they'd moved on to new forms now.

She lunged. He blocked. Their swords met in a clang. She spun, he countered, and then he swept her leg. Imani dropped, and Akeem fell with her. They hit the ground hard, his body over hers. For a breath, neither moved.

She didn't push him away. He didn't pull back. His hand found her shoulder, and she tensed, but not in fear. Her eyes tracked his face, breath shallow, as he lowered his head. Closer.

"Prince Akeem!"

The voice snapped through the air. Akeem twisted, startled, and in that heartbeat, Imani flipped him with a clean move. He hit the ground, wind knocked out of him. She stood over him, expression unreadable.

He sat up, dazed, only for a guard to appear from the far corner, breathless.

"Prince Akeem!"

"What is it?" he asked, brushing dust from his clothes, very careful not to look at Imani.

"There's been a development," the guard said. "I'm to take you to the tech center."

Akeem nodded. When he turned to Imani, she was already moving, and they walked together.

By the time they arrived, the room was full of everyone. At the center of it all stood a sleek suit of armor on a table, with Alkeic stones embedded along its joints and chest. Wings were fixed onto the back.

Akili stepped forward and pointed. "We followed your specs. It's ready for testing. One of the engineers volunteered, —"

"No," Akeem said, raising his hand. "I'll do it."

There was a stir of murmurs in the room. Akili frowned and stepped closer.

"My lord, we don't know what the suit will do yet. It could be unstable. One of us should try it first, and if anything happens, we'll be able to respond quickly. We can't risk you."

"I brought the idea," Akeem said. "If someone's going to test it, it has to be me. I won't stand by and let someone else get hurt trying to prove a vision that came from my mind. I'll be fine. Besides…" He smiled as he glanced at Imani. "I've got the best guard in Alkebulan watching my back."

Imani gave him a faint smile, but he could see the worry behind it.

Akili hesitated, then turned to Shabazz, who gave a nod. That was enough. Akili exhaled and gestured toward the armor.

Akeem stepped forward, and the engineers helped him into the suit. It was light, shockingly so. The inside was warm, lined with a soft mesh that moved with him. It felt less like armor and more like a second skin. When the wings snapped into place behind him, he turned slightly, eyes wide with wonder.

Then, they handed him a sword.

"We'll test the strikes and system responses," Akili explained. "Follow me to the yard."

They led him through a sliding door into a wide testing arena, the floor lined with sensors. Akeem took his place in the center and waited. Akili gave the signal.

Akeem moved. He slashed forward, and something shifted beneath his feet, the armor responding instantly. His steps were lighter and faster. His strikes came smoothly, as if the suit was reading his thoughts.

Then Akili gestured again toward his hip. Akeem obeyed, and his fingers touched a small lever. The world tilted.

With a sudden surge, the wings launched him upward into the air. He gasped, startled, rising above the testing yard. He hovered, then dipped and twisted, feeling weightless. Before he could even shout his awe, shapes flickered into view: holograms, human forms rushing him from all angles.

Akili's voice echoed from below. "Engage them!"

Akeem didn't hesitate. He struck fast, parried, and twisted mid-air. The armor didn't just follow him; it carried him. He fought like he never had before. Then, the forms vanished. It was over.

Applause burst from below. Akeem descended slowly, a wild grin breaking across his face as the engineers helped him out of the suit. Akili was already talking, praising the responsiveness, noting a few calibrations that still needed adjusting. The suit wasn't finished, but it worked.

"You didn't tell me about the wings," Akeem said, laughing, still breathless.

Akili smiled. "We weren't sure it would fly. We decided to try it out."

"Well, I like it," Akeem said. "Let's make it better."

As he left the yard with Imani walking just behind him, the rush hadn't faded. He turned to her, speaking too fast, like a boy who'd touched the moon and needed someone to see it too.

She smiled, only listening. It made him want to say more. To say everything. But first, he needed a shower. Then he'd be ready.

***

Later, as he approached the library with Imani behind him, he slowed his steps so she could walk beside him.

"Your brother is very smart," he murmured.

"He is," she answered, smiling.

"I believed he could pull it off, but not so fast. That prototype felt perfect. Did you see how quick the strikes were?"

"I think it was a brilliant idea. I'm glad it came to life. Now everyone will get to benefit from it."

"And we'll defeat Muovu," he added, quieter now.

They fell silent.

Then he spoke again, almost in a whisper. "And what happened before we were interrupted —"

"No."

He turned to her, confused, searching her face, but she was looking everywhere except at him.

"Imani—"

"I'm sorry, my lord. We can't talk about that. The royal family—"

"I know the words already," he cut in, a little sharper than he meant to. "You don't have to repeat them." He paused, tried to soften. "I just... I know what I feel. And it's real."

"It's not."

"It is for me," he murmured, stepping slightly closer.

"You're only feeling this because I train you. Because we're around each other every day—"

"Imani, look at me."

She didn't answer right away. Then slowly, reluctantly, she lifted her gaze. Her breathing was shallow, and in her eyes, he saw something flickering—something closer to longing.

"If being close to someone every day made you fall for them," he murmured, "then I'd feel this way about Shabazz or any of the other Magi. Even Akili. But I don't. I feel this... for you. Only you."

348

It wasn't quite a confession, but it was close enough. Her eyes widened, her lips parted ever so slightly, and for a heartbeat, everything in him screamed to close the distance between them. But he didn't. He respected her far too much to be careless with the moment.

Then she blinked and looked away, shaking her head.

"I can't," she murmured quietly. "It means nothing. I was just—I'm sorry. I can't."

He couldn't lose her. He scrambled for something she wouldn't reject.

"Fine. Then… then I admire you. You're a skilled warrior. I envy your control, your focus—"

But she was already giving him that look, the soft, distant one that told him no words would change what she'd already decided. Her lips lifted in something like a sad smile.

"Thank you, Prince Akeem," she murmured, and the way she used his title felt like a line drawn in the sand.

He stood there, still wanting to say something, but she went on.

"I would advise you to leave it. You're the prince, and I'm your guard. You can ask anything of me — anything — but not that." She hesitated, then swallowed. "We need to focus on Muovu."

He almost asked her what would happen after Muovu. But the question stayed trapped in his throat. So, he only nodded and turned back toward his destination.

***

For hours, Akeem stayed with Amani, asking questions about the customs of Alkebulan, the things he should already know, and the things he didn't even realize he needed to learn. He asked about the neighboring kingdoms, too, and Amani answered with the kind of rich knowledge only someone who had lived and breathed Alkebulan all his life could offer.

The conversation was almost long enough to make him forget what had happened earlier with Imani, but not quite — he hadn't stopped thinking about it, not even for a moment. And then the doors to the library creaked open, and Akeem looked up, hopeful it was her. But it was her and Kwame and Shabazz, and the look on their faces didn't look good.

"What's wrong?"

Shabazz stepped forward and held out a red envelope. "We got a letter."

Akeem's stomach turned. "From the two kingdoms? Did they say no?"

Shabazz shook his head. "Yes… and no. We received three letters. The first two were from the kingdoms, and they agreed. But this one…"

"Who sent it?"

Shabazz's throat worked. "Muovu."

Amani stood so fast that a book hit the floor with a heavy thud, but no one moved to pick it up.

"How?" he demanded. "Did he come here himself? How did we get it?"

"Too many questions," Shabazz muttered. "It came by messenger who… dropped dead the moment he handed it over."

Akeem stood slowly, his mouth dry. "He died?"

Kwame nodded. "Right in front of us. He had no wounds. Just collapsed. Muovu wanted us to pay attention."

"What does it say?"

Shabazz turned to him. "We don't know. It won't open for anyone else. The seal's bound by spells."

Akeem hesitated. "How do I open it?"

Shabazz extended the letter toward him. "Just take it. If it's meant for you, it will open."

The moment Akeem's fingers touched it, something sharp and hot surged into his palm like lightning. He flinched, but Shabazz didn't react, and Akeem said nothing. He held the letter tighter. It unfurled on its own, as though recognizing its reader. The parchment inside was a clean white, the ink in red, until Shabazz stepped beside him and said quietly, "That's not ink. That's blood."

Akeem almost dropped it, but he held firm and began to read out loud.

"Prince Akeem, last heir of Alkebulan, greetings to you. I would send congratulations, but it would be a waste of words, since you will no longer be breathing soon."

Imani made a sound, somewhere between a gasp and a cry, but Akeem didn't look up. He kept reading.

"Without wasting more time, this is to tell you to surrender. I had the pleasure of slaughtering your father, of sending him to the place he truly belonged, and I can easily send you there too. You've never met him or your mother. But I can reunite you. If you want to stay alive just a little longer, surrender. Or watch everyone around you die screaming. You don't know what pain is. But I will teach you."

Silence filled the room like smoke. No one moved. Not even Akeem

Then he spoke. "We accelerate the plan."

Shabazz blinked. "But the armor — we only just —"

"We work faster." Akeem's voice was calm, like stone. "Muovu already said it. He's coming for us. That's what happened with my parents. They thought they had time. They didn't. And we won't either if we wait. We strike first."

Again, the silence returned. But this time, it was a different kind, one where everyone was thinking and processing. And then, Shabazz nodded once. The others followed. Even Imani.

"This is also the moment to call in the alliances," Shabazz said. "The neighboring kingdoms agreed. We need to act before they change their minds. It's time to pay them a visit."

Akeem nodded, the letter still gripped in his hand. "Whatever it takes," he murmured. "I'm in."

CHAPTER 21:

The Triad Alliance

Their first visit was to Zamunda.

With the help of his aide, Akeem dressed in a fitted black tunic with gold detailing stitched into the fabric, paired with matching pants. Shabazz had argued, insisting he wear ceremonial robes and a crown, something more traditional. But Akeem refused. History had taught him enough. He was stepping into another king's domain, and though he was a prince, he was the one seeking aid. This wasn't the time to measure thrones.

Besides, he wasn't trying to impress anyone. Or so he told himself.

Still, when the doors to his chambers opened and he stepped into the hallway, the way Imani froze made it worth every decision he had made. Her eyes caught on him, and for a moment, her mouth fell open. She recovered quickly, muttering that he looked good, but he'd already seen her face.

The look made it worth getting a proper trim, especially since the only attention his hair had received lately was a hasty comb-through. His beard, too, had finally been shaped instead of ignored.

On stepping outside, the vessel stood waiting. At its base, Shabazz stood, flanked by other Magi. Akeem expected they would all be traveling together, but when he climbed aboard and turned to look, only Shabazz and Imani followed him in. The hatch closed behind them.

He turned, confused. "Where are Kwame and Amani?"

Shabazz adjusted a control on the console, then glanced back. "They're staying behind. The tech center needs their oversight while the armor systems are being finished. If anything happens, we'll return immediately."

"But we're taking no guards with us—"

"Zamunda and Wakanda are allies. And even if one were to turn against us, they wouldn't dare hold us prisoner. Not even Muovu would rob himself of that kind of spectacle. He'd want it for himself." Shabazz offered a faint smile. "We're safe."

That seemed enough.

Shabazz keyed in the destination, and within moments the vessel leapt into motion. Barely ten minutes had passed before the ship began to descend, and through the window, Akeem could see rows of soldiers lined up at attention.

As the ramp lowered and they stepped out, with Shabazz in front, Akeem behind him, and Imani at his back, he caught sight of the man waiting at the head of the Zamundan guard. Robes of deep red flowed over his broad shoulders, trimmed in gold, and on his head sat a crown carved from emeralds. King Joffer.

He approached with open arms and embraced Akeem like he had known him since birth.

"Son of King Jabari and Queen Malaika," the king said in a booming voice, his arms still around him. "You are welcome here."

Akeem found himself smiling despite everything pressing on him.

"Thank you, Your Majesty."

"Call me King Joffer," he replied. "You are a prince and a guest in my kingdom. I see you as my equal." His tone softened. "I already know why you've come. We have much to talk about."

"Thank you, King Joffer."

As they walked through the palace, Akeem let his eyes roam. Zamunda was unlike anything he'd seen in the sanctuary. It was a breathtaking blend of the old and the new—ancient craftsmanship laced with cutting-edge design. Smooth stone walls curved in geometric patterns, etched with symbols that glowed faintly with embedded tech.

Golden archways rose beside panels of translucent metal that shimmered with light, and yet, carved wooden beams still lined the halls.

They reached the council chamber, a wide circular room where light spilled through tall, arched windows made of glass. Four men were already seated—Joffer's advisors. They stood when Akeem entered, offering before returning to their seats.

Servants moved quickly, setting refreshments on the table: plates of fruit, honey-drizzled bread, and something spiced that smelled divine. Akeem didn't touch any of it. He was too on edge.

King Joffer seemed to notice and gave a gentle nod. "Speak freely, Prince Akeem."

Akeem bowed his head in thanks, then raised it again. "First, let me say Alkebulan has never forgotten Zamunda's loyalty. I may not have lived through the past alliances, but I've read of the battles. You stood with us when no one else did, and for that, I'm grateful."

King Joffer smiled, eyes crinkling. "Ah, those battles. You know, your father and I fought side by side once."

And then he began to tell stories and Akeem ensured to laugh and nod at the right time. Amani had told him that when you visited a king, you let him lead the air until he handed it over to you. That was the custom. No matter how urgent your mission, you waited for the moment. It came when King Joffer's face grew serious. He leaned back, the room falling still.

"But I doubt you came just to hear my old war stories. What's your mission, Prince Akeem?"

Akeem met his gaze. "Muovu wants Alkebulan. We have reason to believe he's not acting alone. Also, he's gathering dark forces."

King Joffer's brow didn't move, but something cold slid into his eyes. Then a small smile cut across his lips.

"I expected as much. Especially after the letter he sent me."

Akeem's stomach dropped. He hadn't even thought of that. He'd been so focused on convincing them, he forgot Muovu would try to beat him to it.

"He threatened you?"

"Told me not to help you or I would suffer the consequences." King Joffer chuckled, but it held no humor. "Your father warned me about many things. I should've returned the favor. I once suspected Muovu, but your father... bless him, he trusted too much. I mourn their loss. They didn't deserve what they got."

Akeem swallowed hard. But one answer still hung in the air.

"So, will you help us?"

King Joffer leaned forward, both palms on the table.

"Of course. Zamunda didn't forge an alliance with Alkebulan just to watch a madman tear it apart. Zamunda stands ready to join forces with Alkebulan. Tell us what you need, and it will be done."

Step one. Accomplished.

But this wasn't the end. Before they left the sanctuary, Akeem had spent hours with Shabazz, Imani, and Akili strategizing. If the three kingdoms were to unite, they needed to do it with precision. Akeem's proposal was to attack in waves instead of one overwhelming number. It would confuse Muovu and make him believe they had more armies than they truly did.

Fortunately, they had all seen the wisdom in it.

So, with Imani and Shabazz at his side, Akeem shared the plan. King Joffer didn't hesitate. He would deploy half his forces, which was more than what the sanctuary had managed to raise so far. And if Wakanda joined them too, they could tighten the trap from all sides.

When the final terms were agreed on, King Joffer rose and clasped Akeem's shoulder.

"Once this is over, you must return properly. You'll be a guest of honor."

Akeem smiled. "I promise. I'll come back."

With one kingdom secured, one ally at their side, they turned their eyes to the next: Wakanda.

According to what Akeem had gathered, Wakanda was ruled by Queen Ramonda, daughter of the late King Lumumba. Akeem had been ten when the old king died, so while the queen surely knew the history between Wakanda and Alkebulan, she hadn't been the one his parents worked with. Whether she carried her father's fire was still uncertain. Even Shabazz couldn't say, despite the cordial letter she'd sent them.

Their arrival mirrored Zamunda's: guards, ceremony, and the queen herself standing at the forefront, a tall woman in colorful ceremonial robes. Queen Ramonda greeted them with open arms, her eyes sweeping Akeem with something close to awe.

"You've grown tall," she murmured, smiling. "You look like your father. And your mother too. I knew her when we were girls. It's good to see you, Akeem."

He took it all in. Where Zamunda blended the traditional and the futuristic, Wakanda had machines. The walls shimmered with kinetic energy, and floating drones scanned the perimeter with soft humming sounds. Akeem was wide-eyed but trying not to look it. The queen noticed.

"Let me show you around," she murmured.

He didn't want to seem rude, so he followed as she guided them through sleek halls. He was awestruck. It felt like stepping into the future, yet the future had soul here. For the first time, he felt oddly at home in a place he had never been.

Eventually, she led them into a wide room where her advisors were already gathered. Unlike King Joffer, there were no stories. The moment Akeem finished thanking her for the help Wakanda had shown Alkebulan in the past, she cut to the chase.

"We received a message from Muovu," she murmured. "He threatened to conquer Wakanda if we sided with you. So, when I heard you were coming, I already knew what you wanted."

Akeem met her eyes. "And what is your answer, Your Majesty?"

She looked down at her clasped hands for a beat, then back up. "When I took the throne, I prayed for a reign without war. Peace has always been my priority. We've had our internal problems, but nothing we couldn't fix. Alkebulan... we knew your land suffered. We just didn't know where you were — that child of prophecy." She let out a breath. "But when your letter came, I realized we now know what to do. Now it's time to help our sister nation find its peace."

Akeem nodded. "I won't forget this. Thank you."

She nodded back, and he explained the strategy. He told her how Zamunda would strike first, followed by Wakanda, and then Alkebulan's forces delivering the final blow. Queen Ramonda agreed, but one conversation wasn't enough. In the days that followed, Akeem convened multiple war councils with the monarchs and then, finally, after long hours of negotiation, the pact was sealed. The Triple Alliance was born — Zamunda, Wakanda, and Alkebulan — three kingdoms, three armies, one mission.

They also settled on a final meeting where all three kingdoms would reconvene and align their moves. When it was over, Akeem, Shabazz, and

Imani returned to the vessel. Neither of them said much, but Akeem saw the look of pride on their faces, especially Shabazz. He'd done well.

Imani also smiled at him, and his chest tightened. But he held it down, refusing to let anything slip, at least not in front of Shabazz.

*****

Now that he had both kingdoms on board, the real work began—action, coordination, implementation. But Akeem hadn't forgotten the one thing he'd been quietly building behind the scenes. When they returned to the sanctuary, Shabazz suggested he rest, saying he'd update the rest himself.

Akeem agreed. Not because he was tired, but because he had unfinished business. The system. He was close to completing the hack. He'd set the new firewall but hadn't yet locked out every vulnerability. And something told him Muovu's people hadn't noticed the breach yet.

After freshening up, he buried himself in work. All evening, he worked on tightening the code. By the time he was halfway done, dinner had already been served. He didn't eat a lot, and even Imani seemed to notice. She gave him a half-curious, half-concerned look, but he kept it to himself.

The next morning, he skipped breakfast. He wasn't hungry. Instead, he headed straight for the tech center. As if fate aligned with his purpose, both Shabazz and Akili were there, deep in discussion. They stood straighter when they saw him.

"My Lord," Akili said, "are you here to check on the suit? We've made good progress."

Akeem shook his head. "Not about the suit. I want to show you something that might give us an edge."

They followed his steps as he crossed to one of the workstations. The holographic interface blinked to life. He began entering commands, his fingers flying across the keys. Akili stepped closer, then froze.

"You... overrode the encryption?" Akili whispered. "But this level of clearance—I've never even accessed this part."

Akeem didn't reply. He moved swiftly through the interface until he reached the core display. The last door unlocked. Information flooded the screen in streams of data.

Akili's mouth fell open.

The others noticed the shift in energy and drifted closer, including Shabazz and Imani.

"What's happening?" Shabazz asked.

Akili turned. "Prince Akeem has hacked into Alkebulan's entire digital framework."

A sharp intake of breath rippled through the room. Engineers gasped. Shabazz stepped forward.

"I'm not sure I understand."

Akeem finally spoke. "Every server and data stream in Alkebulan is now under our control. Communication, surveillance, resource logs, power grids... all of it."

"You're saying we own the entire network?" Shabazz asked.

Akeem nodded. "Exactly. At first, I thought we could use it to force Muovu into surrender. But that option's off the table."

Shabazz's expression turned grim. Akili, on the other hand, couldn't stop talking about how he'd never seen anyone override the protocols like that. He even asked Akeem to teach him.

"There'll be time for that," Akeem said. "If we win this war."

But it also meant one thing: Muovu would be furious. And if he wasn't already planning an attack, he'd start now. Time was slipping.

Shabazz asked the question they were all thinking. "What day?"

Akeem turned to Akili. "How's the armor coming?"

Akili lit up. "The integration's solid. The new system syncs beautifully with your neural commands. It's holding better than we expected… But we need more time. Still some instability."

"How long?"

"Three days. Four max."

Akeem faced Shabazz. "Then we hit in seven."

***

Once the date was set, everything shifted. The air thickened with urgency. Soldiers trained harder, engineers moved faster, and Akeem found himself juggling more than ever. He also had to keep up his sparring sessions with Imani.

On all fronts, he was gaining ground, but not with her.

They still shared smiles and brief touches. But it felt different. Off. He started noticing the way she drifted sometimes, as if her mind was somewhere else. He tried pulling her back, but she'd already be gone.

He had to ask one time. "Are you alright?"

She waved it off. "Just tired."

"Then rest," he murmured.

"I'm fine."

But she wasn't. And he knew it. Still, he backed off, unsure if he was pushing too hard.

***

By the third day, the meeting finally happened. Akeem found himself seated in the command tent beside King Joffer and Queen Ramonda. At first, nerves threatened to betray him. He was still new to this, but the monarchs were seasoned. King Joffer spoke with clarity, and Queen Ramonda matched him with sharp insights. They understood the stakes. And they trusted Akeem.

That meant everything.

Earlier that morning, before the meeting was called, Akeem had walked through the resistance encampment. Alkebulan's military base was unlike anything he'd seen—sleek hovercrafts hovered silently above the earth, their surfaces gleaming beneath the sun. Drones hummed overhead, while warriors in armor moved in a rehearsed rhythm.

Now, Shabazz was briefing them.

Moavu, he explained, was not just a threat. He was a disease, spreading his influence across African nations, backed by the dark underbelly of the Global North. The United States. The U.K.,

France, and Israel. They funneled weapons, satellites, intelligence, and money to him. And in return, Moavu promised them Alkebulan.

His image flickered above the map: a scowl so permanent it seemed chiseled in bone and scars carved across his cheeks. Akeem understood now why Shabazz had said surrender would never be an option. Moavu had no intention of compromise. He wasn't fighting a war. He was executing a theft. At the center of it all were the Alkeic stones.

As the stones were capable of storing and releasing energy, they powered the kingdom's most advanced technologies. That's why Moavu had to be stopped, and Akeem already made it his mission.

After the meeting, Akeem returned to his room, hoping to read something he'd been meaning to revisit. But his mind kept drifting. He spent an hour with the text, and then, unable to sit still, he made for the training yard, with Imani agreeing to spar with him.

They were still catching their breath when Akeem stepped back, eyes fixed on her. Imani mirrored him, chest rising, sweat glistening on her brow.

"There's something between us," he murmured.

She straightened. Her expression darkened. "My Lord—"

"Just listen." He lifted a hand. "Don't argue. Just hear me out."

She went quiet, though her jaw tensed.

"I read something," he murmured. "A chapter on the bonds formed between warriors who spar together. Especially when there are... feelings involved."

Her brow twitched, but she murmured nothing.

"I didn't understand it then. But now I do. I've seen it in the way we fight. Your strikes have changed. More controlled. It's not just skill. I feel it and I know you do too."

She shook her head. "No. You're reading too much into it. I'm getting better because I'm training more, not because of... that."

"Because you're training with someone you care about," he murmured, stepping closer. "Because we care about each other."

She gave a dry laugh, but it carried no warmth. "That's bold, even for you. You can't say that like it's a fact. And even if it were, we both know what our roles demand. My feelings—whatever they are—don't belong here. They don't affect my ability."

He didn't flinch. Instead, he reached for the book he had left on a nearby rock and held it out.

"Then read this. Take your time. When we next meet, tell me what you understand from it."

She hesitated, then took it from his hand.

Without another word, Akeem turned and walked away, resisting the pull to glance back. He had said his truth. Now, it was hers to face.

Whatever she chose to give him, he would accept.

CHAPTER 22:

Night of Reckoning

The day finally came.

From morning till dusk, the whole place buzzed with movement. Final checks. Quick drills. Everyone was tense, and for good reason. This was it. Some soldiers volunteered to test their suits again. Most worked fine. But Akeem's was different. His had to be perfect. He'd be at the front, likely face-to-face with Muovu. There couldn't be any mistakes.

At the tech center, engineers helped him into the suit. Imani assisted too, moving around him carefully, making sure it fit just right. But not once did she look at him, no matter how many times he tried to catch her eyes.

Ever since he gave her the book, she'd avoided meeting his gaze. She read it. He knew she had. And every time she ducked away, it was like she was afraid he'd see the truth in her eyes.

She could deny it, but he felt it. Maybe she didn't even know when it started. Maybe it crept up on her, but it was there. And he understood this wasn't the best time. War hung over their heads.

She probably thought her feelings would distract him.

They wouldn't.

He knew what had to be done. But he wouldn't deny what he felt either.

"Okay," Imani said, stepping back. "Suit's ready."

They headed out to the testing yard, now glowing with torches. Akeem ran drills with his sword: quick cuts, sharp blocks, practiced parries. He felt lighter than before. He launched a few feet into the air and spun mid-strike. When he landed, Akili was waving at him to come down.

Akeem dropped softly to the ground.

"That's a big step up from your last trial," Akili said, walking towards him. "We'll make a few tweaks, but nothing major."

As the engineers moved in to help him out of the suit, Akeem asked, "What's the success rate?"

"Eighty percent," Akili replied. "The other twenty will depend on your strength."

Akeem nodded. "That's enough. Let's get everything locked in."

On their way out, he turned to Imani. "One last spar," he murmured. She hesitated but agreed.

At the training yard, he told her, "Give me your best."

She looked uncertain.

"Don't hold back."

The first round, she did and lost. That changed something in her. In the next rounds, her eyes narrowed. She moved fast. She fought like the woman he'd first watched with awe: all fire and grace. He'd missed that version of her.

They went five rounds. He took three. She took two. In the last, they both collapsed to the ground, breathless, laughing. He caught her gaze and quickly looked away before he could say too much with his eyes.

"Let's go to the garden," he murmured. "I want to see it again."

She stood and led the way. The path was quiet. The garden shimmered under soft lights, parts of it glowing, parts wrapped in darkness. Akeem walked to a stone bench and sat down. He motioned for her to join him. She looked unsure, but after a moment, she did.

"It's finally here," he murmured. "The day we find out who wins. Who loses."

"We'll win," Imani said quickly. "You've worked too hard for this."

He chuckled. "That's not always how life works. I had a whole new life in Atlanta. I thought I knew where it was going. Then suddenly, I was here. Plans don't mean certainty."

"Maybe. But if you believe in something, things can still change."

He turned to her. "Do you believe that?"

She went still. Her eyes met his. She knew he wasn't talking about the war.

He continued, softer now. "You used to say I was spoiled. That I didn't know who I was. Maybe you were right. But I've changed. You even said it yourself." He looked at his hands, then back at her. "So I'll ask again. Do you think things can change?"

She lowered her gaze, and for a while, she murmured nothing. Then finally, she whispered, "I'm your royal guard. That's all I'm allowed to be."

"My father was a guard," he murmured.

"That was different," she murmured quickly. "He wasn't in the middle of a war. And people admired the queen. They wanted her to win in everything." She shook her head, her voice a little brittle. "No one's cheering for me."

"I don't want sympathy and neither do you," Akeem said, leaning forward. "That's what I wanted when I first got here when I was desperate to leave. But not now." He locked eyes with her. "I know what I want. And it's you. I like you, Imani. What do you feel for me?"

She started to shake her head, but he reached out, gently lifting her chin.

"Don't deflect. Just tell me. What do you feel?"

Her voice cracked. "What does it matter?"

"It matters. I want to hear it. Do you have feelings for me?"

Silence stretched between them. Then—barely a whisper.

"Y-yes."

That was all he needed.

In a heartbeat, he leaned in and kissed her. Soft at first. No pressure. Just his lips parting hers, slow and searching. She opened to him, and he caught the faint taste of chocolate. She must have snuck it in during a patrol.

But just as he tilted his head to deepen it, her palm struck his cheek. They pulled apart, breathless. Akeem blinked, stunned. She hadn't used her dominant hand, so the slap didn't sting much. But it stunned all the same.

"I can't be a distraction for you," she murmured, voice calmer now. "What I feel doesn't matter. You're going into battle in a few hours. You need to stay focused. Please, forget about this."

He wanted to argue, but then he saw the truth in her eyes. If he fell, she'd blame herself. She'd carry it forever. He couldn't let that happen.

He reached out and touched her chin again. She didn't pull away, but her eyes warned him not to try anything more.

"You'll never be a distraction to me."

He dropped his hand and stood. She remained seated, watching him. He extended his arm.

"Come. Let's go fight for our country."

She hesitated. Then she smiled—just a little—and took his hand.

It was time.

***

The battle had begun.

Just as planned, Zamunda's forces launched the first attack, intercepting Muovu's incoming army near the outer rings of the Sanctuary. Akeem had worried the civilians would be caught in the middle, but the Magi had assured him as long as the battle stayed outside, the people of Alkebulan would be protected.

Now it was their turn.

Akeem, fully armored, moved with Imani, Shabazz, and a small squad toward the vessel. The two other Magi remained behind, alongside Akili, who monitored their systems, keeping Muovu's men from hacking into their comms or taking control. Additional guards were stationed inside, ready for anything.

Inside the vessel, the men prayed. Akeem closed his eyes too. He thought of the Zion Temple and this time, he didn't just pray for survival. He prayed for victory. And if not that, then for Muovu to surrender, though Shabazz had said clearly, "He never will. Don't expect him to."

Moments later, Shabazz turned. "We've arrived."

Akeem stood, heart pounding. But before he could step down from the vessel, Shabazz reached out and placed a hand on his shoulder.

"This is it," he murmured, voice low. "The moment we've waited for."

Akeem's breath caught.

"I'll be with you all the way," Shabazz continued, gripping him just a little tighter. "Your focus is Muovu. That's all and I'll handle everything else. No harm will come to you or to her."

Akeem froze. He hadn't mentioned Imani. But something in the way Shabazz spoke made the truth flicker between them. His mouth opened, words forming, but Shabazz only smiled, a rare thing that softened his sharp features.

"Defeat him. Then you can tell her whatever's been sitting in your chest. But not before."

Gratitude swelled in Akeem's throat, too full to speak. Instead, he nodded, placing a hand briefly over Shabazz's. Then, with fire in his chest and steel in his spine, he stepped down. Outside, the open plains stretched wide beneath a sun veiled in cloud, and standing before him stood ranks of armored warriors, eyes locked on him.

He cleared his throat, knowing the next move to take. He began to talk, "You know why we fight. We're not just facing Muovu. We're claiming our right to live, to lead, to protect what's ours. And we will not back down."

The warriors raised their fists in unison. "We stand with you, Your Majesty!"

Then, a whistle tore through the air. Everyone looked up.

A missile arced overhead, and seconds later, the ground shook beneath a distant explosion. That was the Wakanda signal. It had begun.

Akeem turned to Imani. Their eyes met. He didn't need to say a word. She nodded once. He turned back to the warriors.

"Let's go to war!"

Their answering roar cracked the sky.

***

The battlefield was chaos.

Akeem ran forward, armor singing against his skin. He yanked the lever on his wrist. Wings burst out, and he was airborne.

The world dropped away.

Wind howled past. He angled down, slicing through smoke. Below, steel clashed against steel, screams rose in waves, and fire burned across the horizon.

He landed hard, rolled, sprang to his feet. His blade met the first enemy. Strike. Parry. Twist. Block. He moved like a storm, untouchable.

All around him, his men fought with fury. Then, a voice rose above the battle.

"Leave the false heir for me!"

Akeem's blood iced over, but he didn't freeze. He ran toward the voice. And there was Muovu. Just like he had seen on the holographic display during the meeting, he was tall, broad-shouldered and his face was carved with scars. Their eyes locked, and for a breath, nothing else existed.

Muovu grinned. "Little prince."

Akeem struck. Steel met steel in a violent burst of sparks. The shock rattled up his arms. Muovu hit like a battering ram, every blow heavier than the last.

"Where's Nala's family?" Akeem snarled, dodging a vicious arc.

Muovu laughed. "Dead. The royal aide wouldn't talk, so I slit her parents' throats myself."

White-hot rage exploded through Akeem's veins.

"You monster!"

Muovu only grinned wider. "I wish you could tell her you killed me. But right now, my men are with her." Muovu's grin widened.

"You won't save anyone, boy."

Akeem roared and lunged. Muovu sidestepped, slamming him back. Akeem's foot caught on rough ground, just enough. Muovu's blade slashed across his ribs. Fire ripped through him, but he stayed upright.

Then a scream.

Akeem's head snapped toward Imani, who was fighting two warriors. Her spear danced, but one landed a blow to her shoulder. She staggered.

"Imani!"

Muovu's sword came down, the blade piercing his armor with a sickening crunch. Akeem gasped as the suit cracked, revealing his chest beneath. The force drove him to his knees.

"Fight me, little prince!" Muovu yelled.

Imani's voice rang out. "Akeem, don't stop!"

But his muscles screamed. Every breath burned. Then Muovu raised his blade for a strike and Imani moved. With a cry, she hurled her spear. Muovu twisted, but not fast enough, as the tip tore through his side.

Instead, Muovu laughed. "Pumbafu," he spat, "you trust your life to a female guard? How pathetic."

And then his free hand struck like a viper, a hidden laser gun suddenly appearing in his hand. He fired, the beam striking Imani in her stomach.

"No!" Akeem's scream tore from his throat.

Imani collapsed, blood staining her armor. Around her, enemy warriors closed in, blades raised —

— and then Shabazz was there. A blur of motion, he barreled into the attackers, buying precious seconds. Then, Shabazz turned to Imani. His hands glowed with the pale light of the Ankh energy transfer.

"No, Shabazz, don't!" Akeem roared, knowing the consequences of that.

But it was too late. Shabazz pressed his hands to Imani's chest, and his body dissolved into light, his essence pouring into her wounds. His last words were barely a whisper.

"Finish it!"

And then he was gone.

Something inside Akeem snapped. A surge of power exploded through him, and his veins burned with melanic energy. There must have been something in his eyes as Muovu's smirk faltered. Akeem moved.

Faster than thought, stronger than steel, he struck. Muovu barely blocked the first blow. The second shattered his guard. The third, and then, Akeem's sword plunged straight through the general's heart.

"For my parents," Akeem whispered. "For Nala. For Shabazz. For every soul you ever took."

He twisted the blade. Muovu collapsed, blood spurting from his mouth. For a few moments, he stared at him, distaste over his face, but Akeem didn't care.

And then, silence. Then the battlefield erupted. Alkebulan's warriors charged as the enemy broke and scattered. Akeem didn't look back.

He dropped to Imani's side. She was breathing—barely—but alive. Shabazz's sacrifice had worked. Her wounds were closing, her skin warm under his touch. She opened her eyes.

And then, without thought, Akeem kissed her. For a heartbeat, the world ceased to exist. Then Imani kissed him back.

And in the ashes of war, something new began.

CHAPTER 23:

The Prince and The Guard

The battle was over.

The moment word spread that Muovu was dead, the dark army began to falter. Their swords lowered, and the fight drained from their limbs. There were many — still dangerous — but without a leader, their cause had no shape. The plan was to negotiate. But Akeem had other plans. He wanted to speak. Not just to them but to the people, too.

While the soldiers gathered the remnants of the dark army, Akeem and Imani, flanked by guards, returned to the vessel. The silence between them felt heavy. He tried not to think of Shabazz's absence pressing on him. Thankfully, the journey was short.

They landed in the palace.

The other soldiers — those who had traveled on foot — were sent out with two tasks: bring the citizens to the palace and release every soul Muovu had imprisoned. Akeem wanted them all to hear him.

When the others left, Akeem and Imani were alone. The palace felt like a corpse.

Akeem had once seen images of what it used to be. The palace hadn't just stood with nature; it had pulsed with it. Vines had once curled along pillars, wrapping around polished stone. Light had filtered through crafted leaves of glass. Alkebulan had once mastered the balance.

But now, nothing of that remained. The vines were gone. Statues shattered. Walls defaced. In place of history were hollow-eyed portraits of Muovu, and where there weren't pictures, there were gouged-out holes.

The palace looked like it had been gutted and re-built by a hand that only understood control, not care.

"I can't believe this," Akeem muttered as he sat on the throne steps beside Imani. "We won, but…"

She shook her head. "We'll rebuild. All of this can be fixed later." Then she touched his arm, voice low. "About Shabazz…"

Akeem turned to her. His voice cracked. "He just disappeared. One second, he was there, and then… gone. How? How does someone just vanish?"

"It was the Ankh transfer," she murmured. Her voice broke. "Only an expert can do it only in emergencies. He gave me his life. I didn't deserve that."

Tears rolled down her cheeks. She tried to wipe them away, but her hands trembled.

"I'm sorry," she whispered. "I'm sorry I was the reason—"

"No," Akeem said, pulling her into him. "You're not the reason. He did it because you saved me." He cupped her face, gently brushing the tears from her skin. "Don't cry."

But his own eyes burned.

The truth was, he didn't know why Shabazz had done it. He only knew Imani had been dying, and Shabazz had chosen and had given everything. And now he was gone.

Akeem had counted on his guidance, on Shabazz standing beside him as he faced the people. But maybe… maybe this was what he meant when he murmured some things just had to be done. Was this it?

Was this the cost of becoming the man he was meant to be?

They stayed wrapped in each other, silent, until footsteps echoed through the ruins. They pulled apart as Amani and Kwame entered, flanked by guards.

"My lord," Amani breathed, rushing to him. "You're alive."

Behind him, Akili stepped in, eyes wide, face pale with awe as he took in the shattered throne room. The boy ran straight to Imani and wrapped her in a tight hug.

Akeem turned to Amani and Kwame.

"Shabazz is gone."

Both men bowed their heads. Kwame spoke first.

"We know. We felt it when he used the Ankh transfer. Was it for you?"

"For Imani," Akeem said quickly. "But it's not her fault. She saved me, and he—"

Kwame lifted a hand. "No blame. None. Shabazz did what had to be done."

"But I—"

"No," Amani said. "He made a choice. And he would not want you to mourn him in shadows. He'd want you to rise, live, and lead."

He placed a hand on Akeem's shoulder, and Akeem nodded slowly.

Still, his chest ached. He wanted to ask if there was a way to bring him back, but the look in their eyes gave him the answer before he could shape the words.

Shabazz was gone, and there was no coming back.

"Prince Akeem."

He turned. Imani was on her feet now, held by her brother.

"The hacking is complete," Akili said. "Alkebulan is back in our hands."

Akeem gave a small nod. Then something returned to him.

"The sanctuary... did anything happen there?"

The shift was immediate. Their faces fell. Amani lowered his gaze.

"Muovu's men came, but not for us. They got through the defenses... into the cells..."

Akeem's chest tightened. "Did you..." His voice cracked. "Was she buried properly?"

Amani nodded. "We gave her a befitting burial."

"He killed her family, too."

"We'll ensure every one of them gets the same respect."

That was all they could offer now — dignity in death. And even that felt too little. But Muovu was gone, and Akeem had seized back the power. If nothing else, he would make sure no one else ever suffered like this again.

As if summoned by the gravity of the moment, a guard entered the room.

"My lord. The people are ready."

Akeem turned to the others, and despite the pain, they smiled at him. He didn't feel like a leader. But their faith in him kept him standing. Together, they followed the guard through the corridors to the palace steps.

Outside, a sea of faces waited: faces drained of hope. The air was thick with the kind of silence that came after a storm. His heart pounded. What could he possibly say to a people who had been dragged through terror and stripped of everything?

And then, he felt it. A hand.

He looked down to see Imani beside him, her fingers squeezing his arm.

"You can do it," she whispered.

He swallowed, then turned to the people. The words rose, born from pain and something deeper than duty.

"People of Alkebulan, my name is Akeem, the heir to the throne. The tyrant, Muovu, is dead. His darkness and his cruelty end today."

Some heads lifted. A ripple moved through the crowd.

"For too long, we were forced to believe that power meant fear and that obedience was survival. But we are Alkebulan. We were not made to kneel. We were made to live and to dream again."

His voice grew stronger.

"I vow to you: never again. Never again will this land be ruled by a hand soaked in blood. We will rebuild, not what was, but what should have been. Not in Muovu's image, but our own."

The silence broke.

A single cry rose, then another, and then the cheers spread like wildfire. Akeem walked down the steps, and hands reached for him: hands that hugged, hands that held onto him like he was the proof that freedom was real again. He saw tears on their faces, and he felt something shift inside him.

Now, he understood why he was here.

***

But understanding didn't mean the road ahead was clear. As the people rejoiced, Kwame and Amani quietly pulled Akeem aside. The truth was not sweet. Some of his supporters had been caught fleeing the kingdom, while others remained hidden. Justice, they warned, could not be delayed.

Later that day, Akeem stood in the great hall, refusing to sit on Muovu's throne, stained with the weight of lives taken. Flanked by the Magi and Imani, he faced the former nobles and loyalists who had helped uphold Muovu's reign. Bound and bitter, they knelt before him.

Akeem addressed them, mentioning how they had not only gone along with Muovu's plans but fortified them too. They claimed survival, but he saw self-preservation, not sacrifice. Their excuses rang hollow.

Only one among them dared whisper an apology, but Akeem saw no remorse in the man's eyes, only fear.

Finally, Akeem turned to the Magi and declared, "Let's investigate them. We must serve justice fairly."

The Magi nodded, and the soldiers led the men away. When the doors closed, Akeem stood still.

"I want to see more of the palace," he murmured.

Imani followed without a word.

They moved through the ruined halls. Every room they passed looked stripped of memory, as though Muovu had tried to erase the very spirit of Alkebulan. And then, they reached the royal chambers.

"This was where they escaped from," Akeem said, looking at the wall. "There was a door here, but he caught them."

Imani said nothing for a moment. Then, softly, "I'm sure they're proud of you. You've done what they couldn't."

Akeem's throat tightened. "I just wish we hadn't had to lose so many to get here."

"For the right cause," Imani said, her voice trembling but firm, "people would gladly give their lives for it."

He turned to her sharply, but she was already smiling.

"If I were Shabazz," she went on, "and you were the one bleeding out on that battlefield, I would've taken your place without thinking."

"Don't say that," he murmured immediately. "I never want anyone to die for me."

"But you saved me once," Imani said, stepping closer. "It's only right that I'd want to do the same. I couldn't stand there and let Muovu strike you down like that. And Shabazz…" her voice cracked, "…he didn't just save us. He gave us a chance to live."

Her eyes glistened. "He helped me in ways I didn't think anyone could. I didn't even get to say thank you."

Akeem opened his arms, and she stepped into his embrace, collapsing into it like she'd been holding everything in for too long. He felt her crying against his chest. He held her tightly, his hand moving gently across her back. She had been so strong, but she had also been afraid. And Shabazz had done more than die. He had shown them what it meant to fight for something greater than oneself.

Akeem closed his eyes. No, it wasn't a loss. It was a gift. One they'd carry forward.

***

With the palace now secured and no more reason to return to the sanctuary, they made it their new base. Life slowly began to stir back into the halls. Builders, craftsmen, engineers, and artists moved in, each laying hands and tools on the wreckage.

The Magi, long protectors of the realm's wealth, had kept the keys to Alkebulan's treasury. Now, those riches flowed again. Streets were cleared. Markets reopened. Homes were repaired. And in the first three days, under Akeem's direct command, food was distributed among the people, ensuring no one would go hungry before rebuilding began. Every citizen was tasked with restoring what they had lost, together.

It would not be swift. But it would be whole.

Amidst the work, the Magi brought him news of diplomatic duties. His coronation was soon to come, and he would need to travel to the other kingdoms. Akeem listened, also adding his plans.

His parents once had a dream: unification. He wanted to try, no matter how impossible it seemed.

As their discussion paused, Akeem brought up a topic.

"My father wasn't royal," he began slowly, "not when he married my mother."

The Magi exchanged a glance, then looked back at him. Amani answered first.

"That's true. Is there something specific you wish to ask?"

Akeem's gaze moved between them. He had spent nights poring over the books, and one rule had stayed with him longer than the others.

The guards of Alkebulan were revered, yet they were not nobles. The laws were clear — no romantic entanglements with the royal family. Such attachments, the texts warned, could cloud a guard's judgment, compromise their loyalty, and, in time, bring ruin to the throne. It was tradition and deeply rooted. And yet…

"Can that still happen?"

It wasn't how he meant to phrase it, but it was out now. The room shifted. Kwame spoke first.

"Their time was different. Peaceful. When such questions came, it was easier to say yes."

"I read that back then, marriages between kingdoms were encouraged," Akeem continued. "So, unity could be maintained. But maybe we don't need that anymore... maybe we started well."

Again, the Magi exchanged a look. This time, Amani responded.

"You've clearly thought much about it. It wouldn't be right for us to say otherwise." Then his eyes narrowed. "But I suspect this isn't a hypothetical."

Akeem swallowed. "Imani," he murmured. "The chief guard."

The Magi didn't flinch. Their silence was thoughtful, not disapproving. Kwame, the more rigid of the two, surprised him by speaking first.

"We noticed the way you looked at her," he murmured. "But we thought it was momentary. It's not common, but the world is changing. And we cannot pretend that destiny bends to tradition."

It took Akeem a moment to speak, because the hope that rose in his chest was sudden. Of all people, Kwame's acceptance carried the most weight. He would give it time. But he would plan for it. And when the time came, he would not hesitate.

***

Weeks had passed, and now the coronation had arrived. The sun streamed into the palace chamber, casting a glow on Akeem as he stood before the mirror. His ceremonial robes shimmered in deep purple, trimmed with gold thread.

He had practiced his speech countless times, and now, it was real. He was no longer just a survivor of prophecy and war. He was King of Alkebulan. And as he looked into his reflection, he wished with everything in him that his parents — both the ones who raised him and the ones who gave him life — could have seen him now. Just once more. Just once.

A sharp blast of trumpet broke the quiet, echoing through the halls. It was time. He turned and then froze.

Standing at the entrance, flanked by Imani, now in a flowing cloth — deep red and gold — were two figures he never thought he'd see again, not so soon. His breath caught.

"Akeem!" his mother cried, her voice already breaking with tears as she rushed toward him. He met her in the middle of the room, arms outstretched, embracing her tightly before pulling back just enough to see her face. His father was only a step behind, his smile wide.

"What? How — how did you get here?" Akeem asked, overwhelmed.

The answer came in the form of soft footsteps and the rustle of ceremonial robes. The Magi entered behind them. Akeem turned to them.

Amani offered a smile. "Shabazz arranged it. He knew how much it would mean to you. He wanted it to be a surprise."

Akeem turned back to his parents as his father stepped forward.

"He visited us again," he murmured, "and said everything else would be taken care of. We just had to be here."

Akeem exhaled deeply. He wished he could thank Shabazz in that moment, but all he could do was wrap his arms around his parents once more.

As they separated, he gestured to Imani. "This is Imani, the chief guard. She's saved my life more than once."

Imani's mouth parted, ready to deflect the praise, but his parents had already turned to her, offering thanks. She smiled shyly, seeming uncertain of how to respond.

Then the drums started.

The Magi led Akeem's parents away to their seats of honor as Akeem and Imani turned toward the great doors of the throne room. The music rose, and the gates opened.

And Akeem walked.

The throne stood gleaming at the head of the room, its surface restored from the ruin Muovu had left behind. Rich carvings of the sun and moon wrapped around the high back, and it looked, for the first time in years, like the true heart of Alkebulan.

As Akeem approached, Amani stepped forward with Kwame beside him. Amani's voice rang out as he proclaimed the king's ascension. Kwame followed with the sacred rites, calling on the ancestors, invoking the blessing. And then, before the crowd of nobles, citizens, and Wakandan and Zamundan warriors, Akeem knelt. The crown — gold and sapphire — was placed upon his head.

The crowd erupted into cheers as he rose, King of Alkebulan. Akeem stepped forward.

"Today, we do not just celebrate a coronation," he declared. "We mark the beginning of something greater. Today, we rise as one people. We have fought and mourned and survived together. And now, we build."

His gaze swept across the crowd.

"This unity will not be temporary. It will be a legacy. We will be one people rooted in love, strengthened by respect, and bound by honor."

Thunderous cheers filled the throne room. Then, as they quieted, Akeem's tone shifted.

"There is one more thing I must do," he murmured, and the room stilled.

He turned to Imani, who stood beside him. But the moment she saw the look in his eyes, a flicker of confusion passed across her face.

"Imani," he murmured, "you have been my shield and sword and my strength when I had none. But today, I must relieve you of your duties as royal guard."

A murmur of surprise rippled through the crowd. Imani's face paled slightly.

Akeem stepped forward, and his voice softened.

"Not because you've failed," he murmured gently, "but because you've given more than was ever asked. You've fought every battle, and you've given everything. And now, I believe it's time you rested, not from duty, but from the burden of always protecting someone else."

Her lips parted, breath caught. But before she could respond, the trumpets blared again.

Akeem dropped to one knee. Gasps rippled through the chamber.

Imani's hands flew to her lips as he looked up at her.

"Imani," he murmured, "I stand before you not as a king but as a man. A man who has loved you through moments where I feared I'd never see tomorrow. And I know our customs say kings should marry for politics and for peace. But I have chosen to love not for power, but for purpose."

He took her hand slowly. "You were born to guard me. But I was born to cherish you."

He reached into his robe and drew out a ring set with a sunstone that glowed like fire.

"I ask not just for your hand, but for your heart. I want to share my life with you, not just as my guard, but as my queen. Will you marry me?"

The entire room fell into silence.

CHAPTER 24:

Love, Power, and the Throne

Imani stared down at him, her breath caught in her throat, her hand trembling in his. The world fell silent around them. Then her voice broke through.

"Nakupenda sana, Akeem," she whispered, her tears slipping free. "I love you very much."

The room exploded. Cheers thundered from the gathered crowd. Women let out the ululating "yelelelelelelele!", a sound of celebration that rippled through the hall. Akeem's gaze was locked on her, as if nothing else existed.

With a wide smile, Akeem slipped the ring onto her finger. And in that moment, he didn't look like a king; he looked like a man who had found the very soul he had been fighting for all along.

***

The next day, the sun dipped low, casting a halo over the shores of Alkebulan. The beach had been transformed into something mythical. The ceremony would be unlike anything the kingdom had ever seen.

A golden aisle stretched along the sand, gleaming like a path from the heavens, lined with pale flowers, soft fabrics, and lanterns that swayed gently in the sea breeze. At its end, a great arch stood, woven vines in with gold, veiled in flowing silk. The scent of exotic blooms mingled with salt and wind.

The guests arrived — the women floated in gowns of ivory and gold, their necks adorned with glittering stones. The men stood tall in tailored suits and flowing tunics. They spoke in hushed tones, and every eye, including Akeem, dressed in his ceremonial robes, turned toward the horizon, waiting for the bride.

And then she appeared.

Imani walked barefoot across the sand, her gown catching the light. Her bodice was embroidered with ancient symbols, and threads of gold were woven into her hair. Her eyes never left Akeem.

The music began softly. The waves hummed in harmony as Amani, cloaked in white, led them through the vows. When the rings were exchanged, there was a hush. Akeem's was a band of gold, while Imani's bore a single, brilliant diamond. And then they kissed.

A burst of color lit the heavens, and from the cliffs, eagles soared—winged symbols of freedom and strength.

Among the gathered, Queen Ramonda, regal as stone, sat beside King Joffer. Their presence was proof that three great nations—Wakanda, Zamunda, and Alkebulan—were now bound in hope and peace.

And at the center of it all stood Akeem and Imani, hands clasped.

***

Months had passed since the wedding, and the kingdom now moved with a different rhythm.

At the gates of the royal courtyard stood Malcolm—son of Shabazz—tall like his father, with sharp eyes. He bore the crest of the Magi etched into the leather over his chest.

Akeem had been stunned the first time he saw him. "Shabazz had a son?" he'd asked.

"He was far from here," Kwame had explained. "The mountains took him, and the Magi trained him."

"He's returned now," Amani had added. "And he's yours to lead. He will follow you."

And he did. Malcolm was no shadow. He was a flame. His duty now was to walk beside Akeem across every border and battlefield.

Imani stood behind them, her hand resting over the small swell of her stomach. Akeem turned to her, stepped close, and cupped her face in both hands.

"I'll return with a future worth giving our child," he murmured.

Her eyes shone. "You already have. Now go. Make it real."

He lingered a breath longer, then turned. He and Malcolm stepped into the vessel that would carry them across the continent. And then, Akeem set forth on the most daring journey of his reign.

Across mountains, rivers, deserts, and forests, Akeem and Malcolm traveled. From North to South to West and East, they moved like a storm of purpose. Crowds gathered in villages and capitals alike, drawn by the fire in Akeem's words.

Their journey was not without trials, but it overflowed with moments of revelation and connection. As they met leaders and commoners alike, Akeem sought to forge the United Kingdoms of Africa—fifty-four sovereign nations brought under one alliance.

In less than a year, Akeem traveled to all 54 nations, working to realize the dream of the United Kingdoms of Africa. A universal African passport was launched, symbolizing freedom of movement. A single currency, the UKAM (United Kingdom of Africa Makuta) unified the economies and ensured fairness. A continental army was formed, and Alkala adopted as the common language.

Backed by the wealth and tech of the Triple Alliance—Alkebulan, Zamunda, and Wakanda—Africa began to reclaim its power. Foreign exploiters were expelled, debts erased, and global Africans were welcomed home—citizens by blood, not border.

Akeem's mission reshaped the continent. Unity. Prosperity. Ubuntu in action. By the year's end, the vision had taken root. The Triple Alliance became the spine of the continent's new age. What once seemed impossible had become inevitable.

THE END

EPILOGUE

The cries of newborns pierced the hush of dawn.

In the royal bedchamber of Alkebulan, where sheer drapes fluttered in the warm breeze and the scent of incense lingered in the air, time itself seemed to pause. Soft-footed nurses moved about the room with quiet purpose. Upon the bed, the Queen lay resting, her face still aglow from the sacred storm of birth.

One nurse placed a swaddled infant gently upon her chest. Another laid a second beside her. A daughter. A son. So impossibly small, yet already the most important souls in her world.

And then, as if summoned by something beyond sound, the great doors swung open with a hush of reverence. Akeem stood in the threshold, breath caught, eyes wide.

He had faced tyrants without flinching, walked through flame and shadow, stood unshaken before kings and councils. But this — this undid him.

He crossed the room slowly, fell to his knees at Imani's side, and let the silence speak for him. His fingers brushed their foreheads like a blessing.

"They're beautiful," he whispered, his voice trembling.

Imani offered a tired, radiant smile. "Our children are here."

"They are," Akeem echoed. He looked to the girl. "Malaika." Then to the boy. "Jabari."

To name them after the two who had shaped his path was no small gesture. It was memory made immortal.

But then, a soft gasp from one of the elder nurses. She gently lifted the wrist of one of the twins, eyes wide.

Akeem leaned forward.

There, upon each child's left wrist, glimmered a faint, familiar mark—the same sacred symbol that had once appeared on Akeem's own flesh, years ago.

The Magi, already gathered at the door as if forewarned, exchanged knowing glances. They bowed their heads low. That mark, spoken of only in the oldest scrolls, was a sign. A sign of power. Of lineage. Of destiny.

And in that golden moment, as the first rays of morning crowned the royal chamber, the world seemed to still. The breeze held its breath. The trees leaned closer. The air shimmered with quiet revelation.

The future of Alkebulan had arrived—not with the clash of swords or the sound of drums—but with the quiet certainty of legacy. Destiny, once again, had chosen its heirs.

AUTHORS

Emmanuel and Solange Bope never imagined they would write a fantasy novel. Renowned as the digital marketing, social media, and branding experts of Africa, they have dedicated their lives to empowering Africans across the continent and the diaspora, embodying the ethos of the African Dream. They have cultivated a vibrant community of PALs

(Pan African Lifestylers), sharing their expertise in social media, marketing, and branding. As Pan African Lifestyle grew, it became clear from comments on social media posts, emails, and DMs that there was a yearning for original Black stories representing the global Black community and showcasing diverse narratives told by us, for us. Recognizing this overwhelming demand and the rise of African music and content on social media, Emmanuel and Solange decided to venture into uncharted territory and write a Black fantasy novel, leveraging their love for Nollywood movies and classic African American shows and films.

Hailing from the Democratic Republic of the Congo, Emmanuel and Solange spent their formative years in Canada, where they met, married, and began their journey as life and business partners. With a steadfast commitment to God and family, they transplanted their aspirations to African soil, establishing the headquarters of Pan African Lifestyle in the motherland.

Emmanuel Bope, an astute business luminary and creative visionary, leads PAL as its CEO and co-founder. With diplomas in Public Relations and Marketing Communication and a degree in Marketing Science, he orchestrates PAL's strategic direction with unparalleled acumen.

Solange Bope, a dynamic force of creativity, thrives on innovation and impact, forging emotional connections through brand and narrative. As President and co-founder of Pan African Lifestyle Inc., she infuses PAL's ventures with her flair for style and storytelling. With diplomas in Fashion Styling, Image Consulting, and Marketing Communications, she brings a unique blend of artistry and business acumen to the PAL ecosystem.

Together, Emmanuel and Solange Bope stand as exemplars of Pan-Africanism, prioritizing the development of the motherland while cherishing their roles as life partners, confidants, and parents. Their unwavering dedication to creating a new narrative for Africa through media underscores their commitment to shaping a brighter future for the continent and its people. Today, the Bopes serve as brand and media consultants, keynote speakers, entrepreneurs, and philanthropists focused on inspiring the African Dream.

PAN AFRICAN
LIFESTYLE

www.ingramcontent.com/pod-product-compliance
Lightning Source LLC
Chambersburg PA
CBHW051132300726

48978CB00011B/244